THAT BAND FROM INDIANA

by
Charlie Davis

Photos by
Duncan Schiedt
and other
Friends

Edited
by
Lewis Turco

MATHOM PUBLISHING COMPANY
68 East Mohawk Street • Oswego, N. Y. 13126

Copyright © 1982 by
Charles F. Davis
ALL RIGHTS RESERVED

Library of Congress Cataloging in Publication Data

Davis, Charlie, 1899 -
  That Band from Indiana.

  1. That Band from Indiana. 2. Jazz music—
Indiana — History and criticism.
ML421.T5D4   1982   785'.06'2772   82-12712
ISBN 0-930000-19-6
ISBN 0-930000-20-X (pbk.)

ALL RIGHTS RESERVED
MANUFACTURED AND PRINTED
IN THE
UNITED STATES OF AMERICA
PRODUCED BY
PONTIAC ENGRAVING COMPANY
AND THE
OSWEGO PRINTING COMPANY

To properly credit the many friends, associates and even the occasional "Hi-yah Charlies" entitled to appreciation and thank yous would take a lot of sober recollection, a considerable number of pages and a new typewriter ribbon. I thank Miriam Browne Davis for weeding out items of total recall she considered hallucinations, and also my neighbor, John Clark, who suggested realignments and sectional rewriting while chopping down numerous overwritten passages.

Fellows in New York, Brooklyn, Ft. Wayne and other Indiana towns as well as Tarboro and villages down south contributed stories, some remembered faintly, some taken for granted, while others were set aside labelled "maybees." As a devotee of hearsay, with a fondness seldom outfondnessed, I have included willy-nilly such memoranda in the piece.

Charlie Davis

the way it was....

1	ride 'em train	9
2	fancies of spring	15
3	twelve o'clock for Cinderella	23
4	a what?	32
5	by God he's right	40
6	velvet pants	56
7	nothing except everything happened	71
8	look, look, the marquee	90
9	gettin' smart already	98
10	that flag!	113
11	encore after encore	130
12	mish-mash	148

Roll Call   157

FOREWORD

At sometime or other, the favorable winds of arts and letters must have blown across the Hoosier State, leaving pockets of creative talent -- poets, novelists, and humorists. Such greats as Meredith Nicholson, Booth Tarkington, Gene Stratton Porter and General Lew Wallace left their indelible imprint on the state's literature. In poetry and humor, James Whitcomb Riley, George Ade, Bill Nye and Kin Hubbard were all 10s. Many believe such accumulated genius vaulted Indiana into consideration as the **Cradle of Creative Writing.**

This historic creativity in drama and poetry could not help but rub off on her men of music. Musicians distributed over the state in dance halls, pavilions and open-air gardens struck up the band supplying the stimulus for that most popular of amusements -- dancing. Dancing which demanded suitable music -- music not in over supply but readily creatable. The genius of Cole Porter, Noble Sissle, J. Russel Robinson and Hoagy Carmichael filled the void. They came forward with the classics: "I'm Just Wild About Harry," "Margie," "Old Rockin' Chair's Got Me", "Night and Day," and "Stardust," with enough waltzes to placate the seniors. Once in a while a sleeper filtered into the mainstream. "Dreamy Melody" from up around Lake Wauwasee, and "I'm Just a Vagabond Lover" from the environs of Purdue swelled the repertoire, and "Copenhagen" spiced up the program with some loud, fast, and hot.

Throughout Hoosierland combos large and small played dance tunes with such enthusiasm the state became glorified with yet another title: **The Dancingest State.**

This book traces the evolution of a musical group from its beginnings as a small dance band into a highly specialized performing band, skilled in anchoring forty minutes of live entertainment presented in the movie palaces of the late 1920's. During these years Paramount-Publix packaged such entertainment into Revue Units which travelled a circuit of big-town theatres. These presentations required the back-up of the stage band. **That Band From Indiana** was a leader in this field. It was engaged in an interesting pursuit -- at an interesting time ... with a lot of interesting people.

THAT BAND FROM INDIANA

Front row:
Coofy Morrison .. Reagan Carey .. Phil Davis .. Harry Wiliford .. Karl Vande Walle .. Fritz Morris .. Charlie Davis .. Frankie Parrish

Back row:
Gene Woods .. Ralph Lillard .. Earle Moss .. Ralph Bonham .. Jack Drummond .. Art Berry .. Kenny Knott .. Charlie Fach.

1
Ride 'em train

The big steam engine snorted into Indianapolis' Union Station, grinding to a halt with screeching brakes and whistling sighs. It had good reason to welcome a short intermission, having hurried from St. Louis pulling 11 sleepers, a diner, club car and an added special car for the band. Sixteen home-town lads were leaving to challenge the rocks and reefs of the music business in the Big Town.

It was great to see the large crowd of well-wishers assembled to say a few goodbyes, good lucks, and good healths with supporting refreshments. Many of them had not missed a show since the converted danceband presented a "new twist" in entertainment at Indianapolis' Indiana Theatre.

Hissing steam, firemen shovelling fuel with its coal dust and soot; people milling around; bandsmen piling and unpiling instruments; brakemen with long-spouted cans inspecting the underpinnings of each car squirting oil where needed to prevent the horrors of the hot-box. There was abundant bedlam.

"ALL ABOARD."

The musicians - their wives, their instruments, their hand luggage, and some misgivings - boarded the New York Central's St. Louis Limited. Occasional brown bags were in evidence with proven elixirs - absolute specifics for flu, toothache, and lonesomeness. With the help of the friendly bathtub, the bandsmen had all become specialists in the newly developed art of high-tension beverage creation. Unfortunately, their culinary efforts had not kept pace. They couldn't point to a treasure trove of gastromonic gems, and only "Cal's" hamburgers were recognized classics.

All were bound for the Paramount Theatre where Rudy Vallee had crooned himself into the hearts of Brooklynites. The job of following this popular fellow loomed overwhelming: Fortunately, however, the Hoosiers had one thing in their favor: the "new twist" in entertainment featured at the Brooklyn theatre was not new to them. They had offered their Indiana audiences these stage units for the past two years, and to them it was old wine in a different bottle.

The 1920's had seen an unbelievable growth in the number of new movie palaces, each demanding a blockbusting feature picture every week, week after week: an impossibility for the Hollywood studios. They had run out of Ben Hurs, Intolerances, Madam Xes, and they were lucky if they could produce one new, good, solid money-getter in ten attempts. Managers were crying for help; grosses were sagging. There were nothing but features that couldn't draw flies. Smart operators went into the talent market to engage the headliners, and even the lesser lights of vaudeville, to bolster their grosses. Some heard of the Paul Ash thing in Chicago and copied the idea of presenting these acts in front of the house band - up from the pits, costumed, well lighted, and backed by suitable scenery. The leader of the band was a man for all seasons; he'd not only direct the band and be Master of Ceremonies, foil, or straightman for the comedian, but most important of all, be cheerleader as he laughed, applauded, and thoroughly enjoyed the goings-on, urging the audience to do likewise.

The band therefore took on extra importance. It usually consisted of 16-18 good looking youngsters: above average mucisians, a vocalist or two, featured soloists, and an arranger who could give the songs from the Hit Parade a distinctive style. In addition, the boys from Indiana had memorized forty specialties at a level of showmanship that should guarantee success in Brooklyn. In any event, they were on their way.

Comfortably seated in compartments or sections, windows slightly raised, pillows strategically placed, all those who were present and accounted for felt the uncertain forward lurch of the car.

Evidently the big engine had all it could handle in fits and starts, its drive wheels spinning, steam hissing to get a grip on the rails.. Above the din the folks left behind were calling:

"Jack, don't lose your Bass Fiddle!"
"Good-bye and Good Luck, boys!"
"Don't forget to tell the Governor!"

Karl, Reagan and Gene lost no time in settling in the middle of the car. They were a good saxophone team and a handsome one to boot, each 5'9" - Karl and Reagan fairly slim, Gene on the chubby side. Karl's dusty blond hair with a slight touch of red was always carefully parted, nary a strand out of place. Reagan didn't worry too much about his mop of curly after a quick brush. He was more concerned with how well his necktie properly set off his new Arrow shirt. Gene, who was amazed at such concerns, could not have cared less about hair, neckties or shirts. He was always wondering, "What's for dessert?"

The boys had perfected their solo teamwork, raising their horns in unison when reaching high notes; turning toward each other as if in whispered conversation during the quiet passages. The audiences invariably greeted their showmanship with generous applause, to be acknowledged with gracious bows and well-toothed smiles. They had already taken out their horns on the train and were practicing whole-tone vibratos, trying to get the "wave count" equal to make the chord sound as if it had come out of a single instrument.

Harry and Phil lost no time in falling asleep in the rear slot. Comfortable, using a double seat to accomodate his sprawl, Harry was a picture of relaxation, not moving a muscle - no twitches, wriggles, squirms, only a strange monotone coming from him, and he wasn't playing his cornet. Phil was a contrast: he monopolized *four* seats; his position was not a sprawl - more like a flare. But like Harry, his face never changed expression. The short-trimmed mustache twitched only slightly. He wasn't snoring. His measured breathing was more like the witchity-witchity call of the Common Yellow Throat.

Earle (lambchops for dessert) Moss was back in the club car with a large sheet of score paper, a large glass of iced soda water, and an extra large brown bag. He'd make quiet whistling noises in the treble clef, after which he'd pen down a few notes and complete the cycle with a generous pour from the bag. Kind of a tick-tack-toe: whistle...pen...pour/ whistle...pen...pour. Earl was not mad at a single soul. He questioned Beethoven's beatification as he resolved to score an arrangement without the use of a piano, feeling he could hear a note--and hear it in perfect pitch--with no help from horn or string.

Kenny worked at Earle's side, pen in hand, with a stack of ruled sheets ready to extract the score and produce the individual parts for rehearsal. If he happened to get behind in his job he'd call for Reagan, his assistant copyist. They made it look easy.

The rest of the fellows had a crap game going full blast. It was operated by Jack Drummond, the tall towheaded string bass slapper, doubling on Sousaphone, with a tone like the big Indian's who used to play for Isham Jones. Jack was the perfect croupier. Like the pros, he could take the losers' bets with such skillful grace and ease of motion that he never once lost the ash from his cigarette. Even in this nickle and dime game Jack's rakeoff was considerable, and when the bets upped to quarters and finally paper money, he became the "man to see."

Ralph Lillard, a couple of band wives, and Fritz Morris were deep in thought, Fritz in the deepest. He was in 6 Clubs doubled and worried about the Diamond finesse. If the King was right, he had fourteen tricks. They dearly loved the game; all Indianapolis loved the game, and had ever since two local lads, Edson Wood and Joe Cain had won the National Bridge Championships. These fellows - together with Buck Buchanon, Walter Pray, and Doc Nafe - had developed a respectable bidding system long before Charlie Goren seized his pen. Buck claimed he could make 3 No Trump 60% of the time with 22 points. He also allowed he could make a good living in the Columbia Club's card room, doubling one and two nuisance bids. Several of the band lads learned the game from these experts--a sure-fire way, but quite expensive even at a tenth of a cent. Ralph had no trouble forgetting his drums and Fritz his fiddle when there was a bridge game cooking.

The trainride from Indianapolis to Cleveland was a breeze. The huff-puff of the steam engine, ten cars up front, was almost nonexistent, but the monotonous rhythm of the track had a hypnotizing effect--heavy eyes, considerable yawning, and here and there a snatch of doze. A beautiful, smooth, comfortable trip. Pulling into Albany, all hands were tucked in and dreaming about sugar-plum fairies. At Harmon, the switching from steam to electricity caused a startled, "What goes on?" And then back to sleep, only to be again disturbed as the big train coasted into Grand Central Station and relaxed, the conductors inviting all present to debark in a kind of "hurry and get off...we gotta get this train outta here" tone of voice.

It didn't take long; everyone finally got unloaded, without forgetting Jack Drummond's bass fiddle, and they had a short meeting, agreeing to seek out the reserved accommodations and get settled. The band agreed to meet at the Brooklyn Paramount Theatre as soon as possible, say 10:30 P.M.

The men on the ladders had just finished changing the marquee for next week's show. When they turned on the lights, there it was:

    The Royal Family   *Duke Ellington's Orchestra*   *The Great Rubinoff*

                 CHARLIE DAVIS AND HIS JOY GANG

"How about that, Charlie?"
"Don't pinch me...I can read...I see it!"

That band from Indiana had arrived.

The Tokio Orchestra (circa 1922)
Charlie Davis, piano; Keith Findley, sax
George Miller, banjo; Russ Barkley, tuba
Freddie Hulme, trumpet; Ross Reynolds, trombone
Doc Stultz, drums.

THE SYNCOPATING FIVE
Chuck Campbell, Trombone...Dusty Rhoades, Drums
Mutt Hayes, Clarinet...Russel Stubbs, Piano
Fritz Morris, Violin...Herb Hayworth, Banjo.

2
Fancies of spring

Bige Davis played slide trombone for some years in the pit orchestra of the English Opera House where Klaw & Erlanger presented the great shows of the era; "Chu-chin-chow" with its trick mirrors multiplying the cast into a thousand people on stage; "The Ziegfeld Follies" with the fabulous Anna Held whose popularity would never dim; Victor Herbert's "Mlle. Modiste" with Fritzie Scheff singing the immortal "Kiss Me Again", and "The Red Mill" with the versatile Fred Stone going round and round clinging at arm's length to a blade of the big Dutch windmill. Bige's gangling eight year old son sat in an unsold chair and saw them all for free, developing a fascination for the aura of make-believe that was theatre.

Having finished Shortridge High School, working two years as office boy, billing clerk promoted to machine-bookkeeper at Schnull & Company's Wholesale Grocery, young Charlie Davis was thinking about college - a fellow couldn't get very far without going to college. There were lots of colleges in Indiana: Butler, within walking distance; Wabash, over at nearby Crawfordsville, and Notre Dame, up north somewhere south of Alaska - the South Bend School got reams of press reporting its football prowess. One couldn't pick up a paper and not be bludgeoned with Dorais to Rockne forward-passes whumping Army and all comers. Neighbor Al Feeney, center on the great '16 team, urged Charlie to try for a N.D. scholarship, but with Charlie it was maybe-yes, maybe no.

It was good to listen to Al extolling the glories of the upstate school and only natural that when the Notre Dame Glee Club gave its annual concert at the Murat Theatre in Indianapolis, Charlie Davis was there. He enjoyed the solid singing group. They did "Solito Lindo" in Spanish very well; presented the spirituals "Nobody Knows the Trouble" and "Deep River" with conviction, and swung into "Swing Along" with considerable bounce. A young southerner, Charlie McCauley, did an Al Jolson "Mammy" blackface, encored with a cluster of Dixie melodies and then the skinny kid with the Scottish brogue came on stage. He had it all: kilts, tam-o'-shanter, crooked walking stick, and the brogue getting thicker and thicker as he sang. His "Just a Wee Dock and Doris" murdered the audience; "Ken ye say it's a moonlicht, nicht, tonicht," and his way of handling the crooked stick was born of the blood. It was a pleasure if not a revelation to hear Walter O'Keefe sing his Scottish tunes. He rolled the heavy laden brogue off his tongue like a horn in the highlands. Charlie sat there fascinated. It was no longer "maybe yes, maybe no; he entered Notre Dame University in mid-term.

Three and a half years of college were an admix of delight and difficulty. The necessities of living always poked faces in view to interrupt his study concentration. Tuition, housing, and here and there a meal demanded attention. Charlie's small capital reserve soon gave out as well as the contribution his mother and father had planned by skimping. Next came operation bootstraps. He put together a five piece dance band which luckily became the going thing around South Bend, Michigan City and Elkhart, making ends meet but with little sleep to spare. Nevertheless, at the end of the three and a half years the sheepskin was framed and ready for hanging. It had all come up roses and even though he had learned more about music than about foreign commerce, it was time to strike out for something permanent and quit music.

Along about the same time, Fritz Morris, violinist with the famed Syncopating Five which group continually crossed paths with Charlie's South Bend Tokio Orchestra, in the circuit of proms and cotillions, was thinking in a like vein. Fritz entered Indiana Dental College, embarking on his life-long ambition. Charlie joined the Realtor Building Corp., a Real Estate and Insurance company located in Indianapolis, as salesman, accommodating his mother's and father's fond hope that he would not become a musician. So both Fritz and Charlie kissed the music business goodbye forevermore. But forevermore is sometimes shorter than you'd think. They hedged a little and soliloquized a lot. "It wouldn't detract from our mainline ambitions to play just a little -- get a few fellows together and play a dance or two occasionally." A C-note for a 5 piece band was hard to refuse - it wasn't bad to get a little walk around money once in a while. Such frame of mind had this upshot; Dr. Morris and Realtor Davis decided they missed the excitement of playing dance music...missed the hand clapping after each well-played fox trot and dreamy waltz under soft lights, not to mention the smiles of those young lovelies requesting "Margie". And so they played a bit more than they had planned.

THE "FIRST" BAND
Charlie, Fritz, Waldo Purcell, Lee Ridgeway and Reagan Carey.
At the Spink-Arms Hotel...early '20's.

Enter Mr. E. G. Spink, one of the city's forward looking builders who had recently completed his SPINK ARMS HOTEL, a new departure in hotel styling. He thought it would be profitable to engage an orchestra for dinner music and dancing. Charlie Davis' group was just about the right size, played the right type of music, and should do business for him. Messrs Davis and Morris were getting in deeper and deeper.

The Spink adventure turned out well. A clientele of dance lovers, occasionally sipping the fruit of the vine, filled the small room to capacity on most nights, and the band's take of $1.00 per person cover charge added up to a comfortable payoff. Steak sandwiches were $1.25--well trimmed cuts from the sirloin.

Mr. Spink didn't frown on brown bags. His waiters offered setups and soda for $1.50 plus tip. Prohibition was on the books but that's about all. It was a masquerade that never really caught on in Indianapolis. "Smiling Sammy" did a land office business in grain by the gallon can, sometimes without cutting it. Young folks were experimenting with elixirs, and it seemed some were studying to become alcoholics. Fritz and Charlie requested their lads not to drink on the job. They preached sobriety. They practiced sobriety in moderation.

The spring of 1923 came early, and the operators of a dinner and dance spot made early plans. Otto Wray and Gar Davis owned the Casino Gardens, out north on beautiful White River. It was a great spot and justifiably popular, doing business in both summer and winter, with the outdoor dance floor inviting folks to dance under the stars. The stars and the moon combined with a little music packed 'em in like anchovies. Ott and Gar came to the Spink to audition the Charlie Davis Band. They made a quick deal for the summer of '23.

Casino Gardens ... popular dine and dance spot of the '20's.
North Indianapolis on White River

It was necessary to add a trombone for outdoor playing. The full-throated lower register tone of the trombone, especially when enhanced by a megaphone, stepped up volume considerably, and made six pieces adequate.

The band's drummer, Lee Ridgeway, had been in correspondence with the phone company for some time and gave two weeks notice of his leaving to take a job with Ma Bell. It was necessary to look for a replacement, and luckily one turned up. Everyone was sorry to see Lee leave but glad to get a note from Dusty Rhoades saying he was available.

Dusty was not only a good drummer, but also a terrific showman and singer who had been a sensation with the old Syncopating Five, singing Marion Harris songs better 'n Marion. "There'll Be Some Changes Made" and "That Thing Called Love" were bread and butter. He stole Marion's circle motion with extended arms--effective gestures in putting a number over. Dusty was great, in spite of certain rumors concerning his wife which persisted in following him around. Evidently some guy was trying to steal her and doing a pretty good job of it, and Dusty was supposedly unable to do anything about it. He was definitely going to lose her. Dusty confronted the guy and agreed to step aside for One Thousand Dollars, which the guy forked up without a word of argument. The lads in the band refreshed themselves on occasion asking "Dust, how's the market today?" or "Anything else for sale?" Dusty would only smile and leave them dangling. Nobody ever knew whether or not it was idle gossip, but it was fun and everything was hunkydory with the Band. Only it wasn't.

She was quite a number, that little flapper who made a habit of calling, "Hi, Charlie" while she sat at table #6 drinking Tom Collinses with a lively group--probably one of the best dancers on the floor, well shod, trim ankles, good figure, cute nose lotsa teeth, and a smile that would cause a Jebby to stop and look. It wasn't exactly a clash of personalities, but the next "Hi, Charlie, play 'Tiger Rag'" resulted in a slight questioning frown from the usually jovial band leader. The band played "Tiger Rag" with verve and dispatch--the hottest ever. And when the little gal came up again and demanded, "Play something hot, Charlie," the roof caved in. The genial band leader resolved to have a sometime conference with the young woman - which was a mistake.

A good movie at the Circle, a Persian Nut Sundae at Craig's on Washington Street, and then a moonlight ride in "Beulah", the Davis model T. Ford "limousine" - a delightful evening. Miriam Browne was fond of "Beulah"...thought the crate had class. It should have had class as it cost $750 hard earned dollars second hand, but it was worth it, and did its share in helping two people get better acquainted. Charlie Davis had a steady girl, and Miriam Browne from Marion, Indiana, could hear "Tiger Rag" any time she requested it.

And to make matters more comfortable, she didn't think Charlie was too bad. Once in a while he'd leave the bandstand and grab a once-around-the-room with her. She decided he'd never make a living with his dancing even though he had pretty good rythym and only stepped on her toes once in a while, and she politely refrained from saying, "Play, man, don't dance." She forgave Charlie's dancing deficiency and put him in the class of the possibles. He was tall enough-- about 5'10½" and at 165 was just about right. She wished his nose were not so noticeable but accused herself of jealousy, wishing her own were slightly bigger. She did like the color of Charlie's hair--a kind of medium brown-- but suggested on occasion he get it trimmed and not look so much like a fiddle player. All in all she discovered positive values in the fellow: he didn't chew tobacco; didn't eat with his knife; and often remembered to pass the jelly to her before grabbing it for himself.

The fall of '23 with its heavenly colors loomed as decision making time, with answers that squelched all ambitions of dentistry and real estate. The first problem--concerning personnel--was not easily solved.

Dusty Rhoades, presumably with a thousand dollar bill in his pocket, decided to hop a train for parts unknown. He wasn't particular. Just someplace far, far away. One day he packed up his drums and the rest of his gear, said a few good-byes, and evaporated, never to be heard from again. Unfortunately, the Band was left without an entertainer--the fellow who supplied many highlights in an evening's program. Such void must be filled, and an immediate search was instituted. Audition after audition was held only to discover that good singers were few and far between. A good friend, Hoagy Carmichael, suggested that Fritz investigate a fellow down at the University. Big Ed East had been knocking them dead down at Bloomington with clever material he'd written. Hoagy said the guy played pretty fair piano and could easily learn to strum a 4 string banjo. Both Charlie and Fritz heard him, liked him, and thought to make him an offer, but he was 28 years old. Think of it, the Davis Band with a guy 28 years old. No way! Couldn't have those kids coming up with "Hey, gramp, play Wabash Blues, will yuh?" Regardless, the band hired big Ed East, with delightful results.

He killed 'em.

Now 6 pieces, with Ed East, banjo; Loren Schultz, trombone and Doc Stults on drums. Dusty to parts unknown.

Not only did he "kill 'em," he also gave the band flexibility, enabling it to present a complete change of sound. From the sweet and lovely melodies played with megaphone-trombone lead, saxophone counter melody and violin obbligato, it was possible to change the combination. Big Ed would slide over to the piano, Fritz would lay down his fiddle and do his stuff on slap-string bass, which he had been studying; Reagan Carey doodled on his clarinet with high register squeals and arpeggios, while Charlie did his cornet best to imitate King Oliver. Doc Stultz, newly acquired, bounded on his drums like crazy and kept yakking about something he called "real dirt." The change invariably caught the dancers by surprise as they thought they were in another pavilion. It was quite a trick, this switching of instruments. It took away most of the monotony from the three hours of the same stuff and the final week at Casino seemed like a day. Charlie could hardly wait to see how this stunt would work at the Severin Grille, the band's next engagement.

As spring moved toward summer and schools let out, Miriam Browne was happy to be relieved of her duties teaching third grade in the nearby school, and hating it. She often said, "I'd rather scrub floors."

It must have been one of those nights the poet delights in publicizing: Moon high...stars bright...breeze soft...fireflies doing their thing; scrubbing floors, school teaching and Steinway pianos faded away. The gentleman asked the lady, "Will you marry me?" The lady hesitated; she thought, she hesitated some more, and became even more thoughtful. "No" she finally got out. "Maybe I am in love, but I can't imagine living with a traveling minstrel, not knowing where I would live the next day, not knowing where my kids would go to school Thanks, Charlie, but no."

He resolved to speak to her father, who stood a good 6'2" and seemed 9'. Apprised of the reason for the visit, Barrister Browne assumed the phantom bench and the tone of voice a Judge reserved for sentencing: "Charlie, there are two things in this world I can't stand; one is a musician, the other is a Catholic, and you're both of them."

Bishop Chartrand married them on May 19th, 1924, at Sts. Peter and Paul Cathedral. Fritz was best man, standing tall on the Catholic Altar with his Masonic button shining in the candlelight.

3
Twelve o'clock for Cinderella

The '24 Fall Opening at the Severin found the place jumping. The tables were lit--cozy like--with candles on each linen cloth. The silver had been shined to its highest lustre, and the glassware had nary a spot. Customers were in the mood for dancing, and dance they did. Charlie Davis' 6-piece outfit was adequate. Playing the sweet tunes sweetly, they pleased the matrons, while the quick change to Jazz amazed the young folk. The fast tunes should have worn out the middle-aged gents, but they didn't. What a great tonic and energizer is bathtub gin with lemon juice.

At the far table over in the corner sat Miriam Davis, nee Browne, with a group of friends. She wasn't dancing. She wasn't drinking. She knew why. The bandleader knew why. Nobody else (except everybody) knew why. After much backing and filling about musicians and their travelling, she had finally become Mrs. Davis when Charlie agreed to play ten years and then quit. **Absolutely.** Miriam had laid the conditions on the line. Charlie nodded yes in a flash. Tennyson was right, "In the spring, a young man's fancy...."

Fritz Morris, the band's permanent treasurer tried to keep an accurate count of the crowd, but the place filled to capacity and simultaneously developed an accordion flexibility, which made keeping track difficult; however, Fritz figured he could make a down payment on a new car--his long suffering Franklin was about ready to give up the ghost--but he was due for a rude awakening. Instead of three to four hundred dollars cover charge, he took in less than one hundred. Somebody, somewhere had been light-fingered or had at least proved "the hand is quicker than the eye." Next night he had a doorman collecting the band's end of the take, up front.

Wednesday night brought a familiar face to table #2 near the bandstand. Mr. Dave Coulter, the owner of the Ohio Theatre, looked a little lonely and somewhat out of place. It didn't take him long to explain the reason for his visit. The Ohio Theatre, had not been a gold mine. It seemed to play only to customers who didn't mind a really bad picture, and who joined with the half-dozen others, plus a sprinkling of couples engaged in that age old hands-under-the-coat pastime. It's possible Mr. Coulter wondered if he'd made a fatal mistake in converting his profitable livery stable into a theatre. He remembered the great magnificos, their diamond rings, diamond stickpins, and $1 cigars as he watched them assisting the wasp-waists into his brass-trimmed phaeton drawn by the shiny roans for a spirited drive over to Pop June's Oyster Bar where they would down a couple dozen Blue-points, a thick Porterhouse with a baked potato and sour cream, a salad executed at table, and washed down with vintage Champagne. Ah; Those happy days!

"Charlie, Fritz," he began, "I wish you boys would help me out. Bring your band up to my theatre; give 'em the same stuff you do here, and make yourselves some money."

"Thanks," Fritz answered, "but we told Mr. Stevens here at the Severin, we'd be on hand to play his grill six nights a week all season."

"What time do you start here?"

"Ten o'clock."

"That's easy. I'll have you out of the theatre at 9:20. You play two shows in the afternoon and a 7:00 and 9:00 o'clock show at night and I'll have you out in plenty of time to start here. **And pay you $880.00 a week."**

The chore of playing two jobs was not as onerous as it might sound. The band played only the news reel and comedy slots at the theatre, not over forty minutes a show, four times a day. No one was overworked. Everyone had plenty of time for pleasure---golf, card playing, watching ball games. The boys would never forget the thrill of seeing Babe Ruth hit 3 consecutive homers out of Washington Park in an exhibition game against the Indianapolis Indians. They were so steamed up that they adjourned to the rehearsal room after the game and came up with a head-arrangement hot tune. Little did they know it would someday place in the top ten of Jazz Classics.

COPENHAGEN

Bix and the Wolverines

Words by
WALTER MELROSE

Music by
CHARLIE DAVIS

MELROSE BROS
MUSIC COMPANY
119 N. Clark St. - - - CHICAGO, ILL.

A.D. BROWN ART

PRINTED IN U.S.A.

The Tale of a Tune

The man who wrote the music tells how the tune was born.

by Charlie Davis

Way, way back the boys returned from the wars with the comfortable feeling they'd made the world "safe for Democracy, even though they were madder than hornets at finding they couldn't belly up to the Saratoga Bar and order a draught beer. The young lad, who had finally made sergeant, was happy to lay aside his bugle and pick up his cornet, on account of it had valves, making it possible to play a major scale, a minor scale, flutter tongue, lip slur, and even to do a laugh like Louie Panico in his "Wabash Blues," which Isham Jones recorded along with "The One I Love Belongs to Somebody Else" under Brunswick's Purple Label. (This caused the record buffs to scurry downtown with their 75 cents for the single, while stopping at the 5 and 10 cents music counter to hear the blond piano player demonstrate a new tune by Walter Donaldson, the ever popular tunesmith, always trying to write another "My Blue Heaven," or at least another engaging melody with a lyric that made sense, needing only his name to sell a million copies, each of which would bring the price of a sirloin steak, then 30 cents, should the steak weigh about a pound and boast the same tender quality as the musical gem.) The young composer-pianist George Gershwin had finally completed his massive "Rhapsody in Blue," having scored it especially for Paul Whiteman's grand tour of the United States, the first bona fide recognition of Jazz Music as an art form, leading to its beatification and the crowning of the portly maestro as "King of Jazz," even though he wasn't so considered by the musician's musician. The public at large went along with the coronation and gave a standing ovation to the "Rhapsody" as the Whiteman Orchestra played it at the grand Murat Theatre in Indianapolis, Indiana.

This all happened while, in a little movie theatre on a side street in the same town, a tune was aborning.

This tune was an unusual happening. It was something of a shotgun necessity, and here are the conditions and climate pertaining to its birth. Such record closely follows the life style of the small movie theatres as they battled for existence, competing with the 3-4,000 seaters of the late '20s.

Senior citizens will recall evenings spent in the "neighborhoods" or the small downtown houses that featured full-length films, the news, and a short subject — a comedy or cartoon. This lineup did well at the box office for a while, but as more theatres were built and every other block held a marquee, competition forced the addition of promotional events — Bank Nights, Special Drawings, Give-aways, etc. But the most successful stimulant was not the one-time stunt; it was the engagement of a permanent jazz-band-with-entertainers to beef up the Pathe News. Regardless of distracting music and confusing lyrics, the customers listened, came back for more, and continued to come back through the years 1923 to 1930 when such package of entertainment was the going thing in all the small theatres showing movies in Indianapolis.

Some of the talented entertainers in those days became nationally known: Hoagy Charmichael and Dick Powell, of Hollywood fame, entertained with Charlie Davis' Band at the Ohio; Harry Bason, Jack Tilson and Fran Frey at the Colonial; and Bob and Gail Sherwood at the Apollo. Folks will remember Bob Sherwood laying his trombone aside and giving out with his magnificent baritone voice which could render the open "o" better than any singer of songs either before or since. The resonance of his "alone", "hope," "only," or "hold" would have eminently pleased the poets who penned those lyrics.

Our Charlie Davis Band was under contract to Mr. Dave Coulter, the daring entrepreneur who had turned a former livery stable into the Ohio Theatre. Fortunately, there lingered no traceable cachet of the stable except on occasions when the feature picture exuded an unhappy bouquet and required the hurried genius of the advertising copywriters to come with such teasers as, "Hear Charlie Davis' Band with Dick Powell singing 'My Blue Heaven,'" or "Charlie Davis presents Hoagy Carmichael who will astound you with his piano."

And so we played and sang our merry way through slapstick comedy, cold waves in Alaska, and ghost-written political speeches, paying little or no attention to whatever flicked on the screen. Our one king-sized faux pas happened when the projectionist inserted a new film clip into the News without telling us. The scene, a shot of the funeral cortege of a beloved member of the Supreme Court, caught us playing the last chorus of "Tiger Rag" MM220 and fff.

Can't say I blame Walt Hickman of the Indianapolis Times for his blistering comment on our scoring practices. He said we ought to take up plumbing. Fortunately, such errors were few and far between, and, happily, not fatal. The manager and people alike forgave us any conflict in good taste that might exist between the subject on screen and our enthusiastic accompaniment. But our show wasn't an accompaniment at all; it was a separate entity, the main event. The picture was grinding away, and if the folks chose to watch it — it was their business.

Faced with the strong competition of the big first-run epics — "Intolerance," "Shepherd of the Hills," "Cleopatra," and the rest of the sensationals, the small houses could not be faulted for stressing the "live" entertainment feature of their programs. Singers, instrumentalists, and comedians became popular — creating their own audiences — fans who were loyal — fans who claimed their favorites were the greatest — but fans who expected new tunes, new rhythms, and new styles. They wanted to be surprised every time they came to the theatre.

A fresh menu every week became quite a programming chore. Fortunately, our band had a library full of popular songs, but we were woefully short on "hot" tunes. We needed them for change of pace. We played "Royal Garden Blues," "Tin Roof Blues," and "Maple Leaf Rag" until we nearly wore out the papers, and then wondered where the next "shaker-upper" was going to come from.

Often we resorted to "head arrangements" to fill the spot: you take B flat . . you take F. . .you doodle around on the C7th for a couple of bars. . .you fill in the whole notes with tail-gate trombone. . ."Ole, be a hero, give us a 4-bar bass solo." Do .. re, mi sol, do. . . .until every man knew what and how he was expected to play. Such concoctions were almost total improvisations; some were not bad, some just all right, and some awful.

Except on one occasion.

One of these arrangements turned out surprisingly good — good enough for several repeats, and it grew more engaging as we replayed it. It seemed to jell with repetition and, during the second week, we even managed to play it twice or even three times exactly the same as the first, which was not the easiest thing to do with no papers on the music stand.

We were happy to have a new tune in the "hot" classification — one we could use from time to time. This one had a certain "ride" about it that the folks seemed to like and applaud on occasion. There was a little 4-bar chord progression that caught the fancy of the musicians. J. Russel Robinson, the Dixieland Pianist, writer of "Margie," said, "Goddam, I wish I'd written that."

Strangely enough, we were getting requests for the "tune without a name" that had the sousaphone solo — unusual because most requests were for vocals or hit tunes. The most exciting request came after we'd played it with extra enthusiasm just before the dinner break the following Friday. A small group of lads barged down front with a stream of stage whispers one could hear for a city block, "What's that one? Do it one more time." Which we did. One of the lads introduced himself, "My name's Jimmy Hartwell. I play clarinet with the Wolverines."

Jimmy introduced the others: Dick Voynow, piano; George Johnson, tenor sax; Bobby Gillette, banjo; Min Leibrook, bass horn; Victor Moore, drums; and Bix Beiderbecke, cornet.

They had just finished a gig at a dance palace over in Hamilton, Ohio, reportedly causing a sensation with their version of New Orleans Jazz, but one look at them suggested the engagement had not been a financial triumph. They were a hungry lot — sleepy, thirsty, and broke.

Our boys were happy to steer them into Blacker's Chili Parlor with a nod to Mr. Blacker, who understood. He'd let them "eat up a storm" and put it on our tab. We slipped them some walk-around money, a heroic crock of Jasper Corn, and got them a place to stay. The Wolverine lads appreciated the bail-out and they insisted on thanking us again, and again brought up the subject of our new hot tune.

Bix Beiderbecke said he was fascinated with the "ride" rhythm of the piece and wondered if his group might take it over to Richmond where they had a recording date at Genett. I told him, "Sure, take it along. . .do anything."

"Has it got a name?" Bix asked.

"No," I said, "but we'll give it one."

Bix was delighted; he wanted to cut the tune on the flip side of Hoagy's "Riverboat Shuffle."

We should have agonized for at least a respectable time over the problem of the name, but we didn't. Big Ed East, our singer of funny songs, accidently latched onto one that suited everybody. And he did it with great ease.

We thought he was daydreaming as we noted his fascination at the actions of Ole Olsen, our bass player. The "Swede" sat with his sousaphone draped around him, getting himself primed for his solo chorus in the "tune." It was probably the first time this unappreciated instrument had ever been featured, and he was ready to play his heart out.

But he was doing something else that engaged Big Ed's attention.

He was fiddling with a small tin box. It was round and filled with a black mass of something. He had carefully selected a generous pinch and was in the throes of implanting it under his lower lip when Big Ed caught the name on the box.

The roof almost caved in when his voice boomed out "Copenhagen." And the tune had a name.

Some months later, we received a phone call from a fellow in Chicago — a publisher, one Walter Melrose — who wanted to know if he might write a lyric to "Copenhagen" and publish it. He represented himself as the proprietor of Melrose Publishing Company of Chicago, and gave adequate references. He'd heard the Wolverine record and said it was fantastic. We later agreed. The Wolverines made that tune jump right off the wax. George Johnson's tenor sax chorus was a classic — an improvisational gem that might well have been reason enough for 48 different bands to record "Copenhagen" over the years. Large bands, small bands, two or three member combinations with or without vocalists played it, recorded it, arranged it, rearranged it, played it in concert, and finally squired it into its rarefied niche in the Jazz Hall of Fame. Brian Rust, the English discographer, placed it in the top ten of his favorites.

Those responsible for the tune's presence in such select company make an endless list: Bix, George, Benny G., and on and on.

Twenty-eight years after its publication, "Copenhagen" was chosen for the flip side of Theresa Brewer's "Music, Music, Music."

No doubt, everyone is a sometime Cinderella, and like Cindy, the Davis Band never had it so good. Prospective recordings by such outfits as Don Bestor's and Ted Fiorito's of Chicago gave "COPENHAGEN" the earmarks of a hit. Fletcher Henderson with Louie Armstrong's fabulous trumpet solo was more icing on the cake. Things were leaping forward in the fortunes of Charlie Davis and his Band. Business at the Ohio was more than satisfactory, the 800 seat Ohio sometimes outgrossing the 3,000 seat Circle, the Severin Grille packing them in, and with "COPENHAGEN" records to be on the shelves any moment, it was a case of roses, roses, roses. But the clock invariably strikes twelve. Setbacks, embarrassments, and annoying problems were in the offing.

When the Wolverines did their recording stint over at Richmond Indiana, they no doubt had passed the word to the Gennet Company that the Charlie Davis Band in Indianapolis would be a good prospect for future recordings. One of their vice-presidents agreed, having danced to the outfit at Casino Gardens. His wife had told him she'd never danced to a better band, and she recommended that he grab them before somebody else did. But these folks had heard the Davis Band on Saturday night when the Casino crowd was well fortified with homemade restoratives, when the stars shone their brightest, and when the band reached the height of its vigor.

The recording date was a disaster. No crowd of happy dancers, no gushing lovelies with their requests, no shining stars in the moonlight, only that monster horn sticking out from the wall, scaring everyone to death and daring the musicians to play well or else. Pity the poor horn. It couldn't help anybody in any way. It could only deliver to the wax what the Band played into it, and the boys played into it whatever came into their heads.

There'll Be Some Changes Made was the most popular of the day's dance tunes. It was the Band's hit of hits, the tune most requested, the one that drew the most dancers to the floor, and the tune that finished with the greatest greeting of applause. That horn heard the Band play it, and the playback sounded like a mish-mash. No one remembered how he played his part at Casino Gardens for the enthusiastic dancers. It was tame, disoriented and godawful. The next try was more of the same only worse; everyone played the lead. Three more takes and the technician gave up. The Charlie Davis Band had come unprepared for recording. "Boys," the gentleman said, "come back again sometime with some notes on some papers."

Fritz and Charlie traveling together on the return to Indianapolis discussed the path the band would follow in its future. "Charlie," Fritz said, "we are a *see* band - the audience likes to watch this band as much as it likes to *hear* it. I think the market is crowded with *hear* bands and it's no great sweat to organize one, but our bottom line will do better if we go in the direction we're heading. Let's keep on trying to develop a great Theatre band with entertainers, soloists, excellent accompanists, and a group that can hold an engagement for seasons on end and not have to move around from job to job."

The "Disaster" recording outfit. Titled "Music in all directions."

4
A what?

    The 1924 Junior Prom at Butler University was to leave all other proms, cotillions and senior balls completely in the shade. Those that predated it were to be forgotten. Those which would come after would not dare to cast a backward glance. The favors were exquisite, the invitations hand-engraved, deckel-edged on sepia with warm brown ink. The Prom Queen and her court were the loveliest ever chosen. Mothers had spent weeks of seaming, gathering, draping, and fitting to produce tasteful costumes for the occasion. Having given the undertaking considerable thought beforehand, they sought adornment, not tinsel - just simple dresses that enhanced their beauty without presenting the girls as walk-on models in a fashion line.
    The event was to be held in the two ballrooms of the Indianapolis Athletic Club. It called for two orchestras; the Charlie Davis Band, having been granted a one night leave of absence from the Ohio, would play in the large banquet hall and were to supply another combination for the Green Room.
    Fritz Morris had tried to get the Miama Lucky 7, but they were engaged to do a job down in Louisville. He asked Hoagy to get a band together, but he had exams and was playing a dance at the Kappa Sig house. Hoagy suggested the Wolverines. "They'll play like nobody you ever heard. I guarantee they'll knock 'em dead." Fritz decided to take a chance. He'd never heard the Wolverines play. The only thing he knew about them was that they came to Indianapolis from Hamilton, Ohio, tired, hungry, and broke. Having just finished a gig in some dime-a-dance place over in Hamilton, they'd been something less than a financial success, though a sensation musically. Fritz took them into Blacker's Chili Parlor

next door, telling Mr. Blacker to feed 'em and put it on the tab. The band fellows took up a collection to furnish some walk-around money, gave them a healthy crock of Jasper Corn, and found a place they could stay.

The Prom's 9:00 p.m. starting time found the Athletic Club well crowded. Scores of white-ties-and-tails, here and there a tuxedo, and three or four Lieutenants in full parade dress vied with long dresses - prints and velvets of all colors - to give the room the appearance of a flower garden in early springtime. The society reporters from the local newspapers, all pencils and cameras, fluttered about busier than working bees. Everyone awaited the lowering of the lights.

The Davis Band started the evening with some misgivings. The large banquet hall was exactly that--large. Whether a six-piece band would be heard over the shuffling of dancing feet and the natural buzz of the crowded room was something to be concerned about. The Band brazened it out and gave it everything. Charlie wished he was playing with 5 brass-three trumpets and two trombones would be just fine. The boys wished for a tuba or string bass to help out, or that the room would get a little smaller, or some of the dancers would go home; but even so, some things didn't sound too bad, especially when Loren stuck his trombone into the megaphone playing the lead with Reagan duetting it on Sax and Fritz topping off with a good obbligato. Doc Stultz was always there with a heavy drum beat, and with Big Ed and Charlie thumping out rhythm on banjo and piano the dancers had to be held in cadence unless they all had two left feet.

The first number, "The Best Things Of Life Are Free," one of the top tunes of the season, had a few dancers singing, and the tune finished to light applause. The house didn't exactly come down. Prof. Plante came up and requested "The Sweetheart of Sigma Chi" and it sounded good. Mrs. Plante thanked Charlie and Charlie thanked her for thanking him. Ed East finished the set, doing the elephant number, "Louise, Louise, Come Out Among the Trees." The tune always got some laughs from those who didn't dance; the others walked off the floor but came back when the second set started. "Paddlin' Madeline" was a little thin but danceable, and after "There'll be Some Changes Made," with Reagan doing his smothering chorus, it looked like the band might have a chance of getting through the evening.

Min Leibrook
Bass
Dick Voynow
Piano
Bix Beiderbecke
Cornet
George Johnson
Tenor Sax
Jimmy Hartwell
Clarinet
Bobby Gillette
Banjo
Vic Burton
Drums

Bix and the Wolverines

And then the Green Room started to simmer. The Wolverines had just spun into "Jazz Me Blues," and folks were moving there in waves. The introduction and first chorus grew gradually into a stomp and from there it started jumping. Dancers stopped dancing. They rushed the bandstand--a typical bum's rush. The big room emptied; the velvets, prints, tuxes and tails crowding the Wolverine bandstand. The Charlie Davis boys were in the front crush. The room started rocking as no room ever rocked. Every tune added to the frenzy of the crowd. Jimmy Hartwell played a few doodles upstairs--the crowd applauded. Bobby Gillette strummed some solo notes on his banjo - cheers went up. And then Bix Beiderbecke did his break in a repeat of "Jazz Me"— the crowd went wild. Little did they know that break would be copied by every cornet player from here to Moosejaw, including the legendary Red Nichols.

The Davis Band played no more for dancing that evening; there was no one to play to.

Doc Stultz, a drummer with a lexicon of his own remarked, "Man, those guys can sure play that dirt." Dirt, according to Doc, was the highest accolade, and it could only be used to praise the purest quality Jazz Music. He classified this music on a scale of 1 to 10, starting with Nuthin' Music, Tinear, McKinley Stinker, Pantywaist, and so on up to real Dirt. He 10'd the Wolverines after hearing them do "Sweet Sue."

Bix never played a greater one! With a long line of sensational hot choruses behind him, this one topped them all. The crowd stood spellbound by the spellbinder.

"Bix," someone screamed, "that was the most fantastic chorus ever played on a cornet. Please play it again!"

"Impossible. I was lost," Bix retorted sheepishly.

Lost or not, the Wolverines really had it that evening. The crowd stomped, whooped and hollered at every move they made, every chorus, every break, it made no difference – they were fabulous. Fritz and Charlie agreed, "we made a mistake, these guys'll run us out of town."

But Charlie and Fritz had other worries. Nobody knew how they got into the bind, but someone must have promised Ott Wray and Gar Davis that Charlie would play Casino Gardens' outdoor summer program. They were depending on it. At the same time Harry Page had the band on a signed contract to play his Fairview Dime-a-Dance Gardens. Two jobs and only one band. The impressive performance of the Wolverines at Butler's Prom might solve the problem at hand.

"Could be," nodded Big Ed. "They might knock 'em dead."

"Gar will beat our brains out if they don't draw well," countered Fritz.

"Let's talk to some of the customers," Loren suggested. Which they did.

Surprisingly, the reaction was mixed. The Charleston specialists (the band called them flappers, jumpers or jivers) answered with a gush, "Wonderful." Their partners agreed, "Real George." One of the older fellows remarked, "Big crowd, fine; how about tomorrow night, small crowd?" And two professors, both good patrons of the casino, shook their heads, "They wear me out."

But Charlie felt under considerable obligation to Bix and the lads because of their recent cutting of "Copenhagen." They had done a marvelous job on the recording. With Hoagy's "Riverboat Shuffle" on the flip side, it should do land office. Hoagy's insistence that the Wolverines were out of this world and would be a positive sensation at the Gardens swung the balance in their favor, and Gar and Ott hired them for the summer. Everyone wished everyone else good luck, good health and a pleasant season.

The Charlie Davis Band went over like a house afire up at Fairview Gardens. The weather stayed beautiful most of the early summer, and open-air dancing grew in popularity, giving the owner Harry Page, a start on his best season. Ralph Dumke, one of Charlie's N.D. roommates joined the band with his beautiful lyric tenor voice. Teamed up with big Ed and the band's smooth rhythms he helped considerable in rounding out an entertaining program that drew funseekers from all over. From the first lively set to the final *I'll See You In My Dreams,* the turnstiles clicked with dime tickets. Harry Page wore his biggest smile trudging to the bank on Fridays.

Even so, quitting time around midnight was always welcome. Everyone in the band made a beeline for Rochester where Orin Karn's lunch room served the most delicious hamburgers--the only hamburgers ever tasted that could hold a candle to Cal's in Indianapolis. Orin Karn would never divulge the secret of their flavor. Fritz Morris thought they might have had a trace of pork mixed with the ground chuck. Panbroiled in their own juices, they were well worth the two mile trip even if one had to walk. With a dollop of Belgian mustard along with the salt and pepper, one was introduced to the fascinating taste of *sweet and sour,* when munching the sandwich in tandem with a scoop of ice cream smothered in chocolate sauce. Oh happy day!

One midnight toward the last of August something was different. Over Rochester way a red flame pierced the sky, and it wasn't sunset. The town must have been on fire. But no, the source was easily traced to a large clearing halfway between the lake and Rochester. There were thousands of people in white, some on horses, some on a platform, some just wandering in no special direction. They were listening intently to some goings-on. A huge cross topped the hill toward the lake. An awesome sight, the cross smoked and burned, its flames reaching higher than the tree line. Were these people out of their minds to stage this affair so close to the spruces and hemlocks? Luckily, the volunteer fire department was on standby. Indianapolis' most eloquent lawyer was on the platform, being introduced by an important looking fellow with glasses. One had to wonder why Charlie O, a highly respected lawyer, lots of friends, lovely family, and a home in Irvington--why was he involved with this outfit?

His clear voice rang out with a strange plea to the crowd:

"Every criminal, every gambler, every thug, every libertine, every girl-ruiner, every homewrecker, every wife-beater, every dope-peddler, every moonshiner, every crooked politician, every pagan priest, every shyster lawyer, every K. of C., every white slaver, every brothel madam, every

Rome-controlled newspaper, every black spider, is fighting the Klan. Think it over.
'WHICH SIDE ARE YOU ON?"

At the end of his speech, it was not difficult to note the effect his silver tongue had on the bystanders. If America needed to be protected from "Niggers", Catholics, and Jews, everyone should be for it.

Mir Davis couldn't believe she was hearing Charlie O. mouthing such garbage. Ralph Dumke in the back seat agreed with her and suggested we hasten to Orin Karn's. Ralph did, however, give out with some little known information about the leader of this white-masked group. He'd heard from good authority that one D.C. Stephenson, supposedly the ringleader in Indiana, could slip into his white robe and lead a bunch of new Klansmen into a church and pray devoutly with the congregation, invariably presenting the minister with an envelope containing a hundred dollar bill, and take new applications on the way out. Ralph said Stephenson was making a ton of money, selling memberships at $10.00 and even $25.00, plus $6 for the regalia - which had cost him only $1.75. Stephenson amassed a considerable fortune in nothing flat. For some reason, the Hoosiers were ripe for investing in his promotion. When he turned his machinations toward politics he found he could slip into a town, with a pocket full of money, corner enough votes to swing a close election, and walk out with a legislator in his pocket.

Such doings, such a situation, and such obvious gullibility in the people of the Hoosier State gave Miriam and Charlie Davis to wonder. Was this where a young, ambitious Catholic family should plan to settle permanently?

They needn't have been overly worried. "I Am The Law" Stephenson began taking himself progressively more seriously to the extent that he allowed as how he could get away with anything...including murder 1. Not so. In a show of supreme egotism he tried to brazen out a case of criminal neglect which had caused the death of a girl he had violated. The Courts in Indiana placed him behind bars in Michigan City for life.

Meanwhile, the band was as popular as ever at Manitau. Everything was coming up roses when out of the blue came Gar Davis's voice on the phone from Indianapolis: "I'll murder you guys!" (He didn't need the phone, he was yelling so loud.)

"Get me a band, and get it down here quick! We got no customers!"

"You've got a great band in the Wolverines," Fritz yelled back at him. (Fritz could yell as loud as anybody.)

"They don't draw flies. Customers, that's what we want, guys that pay the cover charge. We don't need the visiting musicians that sneak in and listen for free."

"O.K." Fritz gave up. "We'll talk to Doc Peyton or the Miami Lucky 7 about helping out." Both Doc and the 7 had good reputations and were drawing cards throughout the vicinity. Luckily, the 7 were able and willing to come to the Casino and get Fritz off the hook.

Amazing! It seemed next to impossible that the sensational Wolverines had not become the fairhaired boys of the Indianapolis dancing public.

There was no question about the uncanny ability of the Wolverines to please the musicians. These fellows marvelled when Jimmy Hartwell noodled a clarinet chorus. They marvelled when George Johnson knocked off something on his tenor sax; in fact, they marvelled at anything the Wolverines did - no question they were a great band. No question they murdered Charlie's Band at Butler. No question the kids thought they were the greatest. Why then did they fall on their faces at the Casino while Charlie and his boys were knocking them dead at Manitau? Where are the Charleston dancers that went for them in such a big way? Where are the kids that thought they were so great at the Prom?

Fritz wondered about the same sound coming at the customer tune after tune. He wondered about change of pace. Is the guy who wanted a waltz mad as a hornet when he doesn't hear one played slow and dreamy? Then there was the question of inspiration. The bigger the crowd on Saturday night, the hotter the music.

Reggie Duvall, the elder statesman of Indiana Jazz, was a true believer in built-in inspiration and made sure of it when he quoted prices: $6.00 per side man; $10.00 for the leader, and 2 quarts of Gin. You'd be surprised how much inspiration a guy could get out of a couple of slugs of Gin.

But, again, this gets back to the haphazard: how big the crowd, how strong the inspiration, what proof the Gin?

Harry Page designed his new open air "Dime a Dance Pavilion." A knockout.

"Tell Charlie to cut the dances to a minute and three quarters."

5
By God he's right

Charlie and the boys came back from Manitau in high spirits--high, that is, until they ran across Dave Coulter. Usually grinning and ready with a new joke, the Irishman was effervescence in reverse. The boys wondered if the Ohio had burned down? Mr. Coulter said it hadn't, but might just as well have. Business was louzy. People wondered when the band would be back, which caused Charlie to have a misgiving or two and some wonder of his own. He didn't doubt his band could continue presenting interesting tunes, well arranged, and well played; but what about the law of diminishing returns? The textbooks claimed people get tired of the same bill o'fare.

Everybody had ideas, none of them good — except one. The fellow who took "Copenhagen" Ole Olsen's place on sousaphone came up with something fresh. Dwight Jones, not only played good horn, but also was a handy fellow to have around. He suggested, "Let's do a Paul Ash."

Wrinkled eyebrows, "A what?"

Dwight had recently come home after a prolonged stint in Chicago where he had watched a subtle upheaval in the field of live entertainment. Supplementing the screen fare in a downtown theatre was a group under the baton of a very resourceful fellow.

The Paul Ash Story leaps right out of Horatio Alger.

Seeing the failing popularity of vaudeville, the end of the two-a-day houses, the "at liberty" ads in *Variety*, and many top-notch performers willing to accept salaries considerably lower than their established ones, noting the success small theatres in Indianapolis and other cities were having by adding jazz band music, singers, and entertainers to their regular program, Mr. Ash came up with an idea, a simple one: a re-staging the vaudeville show by presenting the acts in front of a stage band with the leader acting as Master of Ceremonies. Ash was made to order. The perfect M.C. He was a distinctive looking six-footer with a mop of darkish auburn hair that blossomed from the back of his head as if teased; a husky penetrating voice that projected anywhere in the theatre, and a smile that said, "I want you to like my show, but if you don't like it at least like me, will yuh?"

His friends from the west coast remembered him as a drummer who always stood out from the orchestra as he whacked away at his drums, smiling here and there as if he were grateful that everyone came in to see him. When he tossed a drumstick up in the air and caught it, he got some hand clapping, and when he missed, he got laughs.

Whether Paul Ash invented the Stage Band Show or it just invented itself will always be moot. Everybody and his brother laid claim to the invention. Every band leader with a girl singer, every theatre having a spare spotlight that a local quartette could sneak into for four minutes, and every ham who could sing "Me and My Shadow," tell a joke or two, and exit with a cakewalk, waving his tophat, claimed source credits. But in the final analysis, Paul Ash in the old broken down Mc Vickers Theatre squired the Stage Band Presentation into the mainstream of popularity that sold tickets by the basketful.

The Ash Stage Band was a galaxy of the finest instrumentalists available with 5 brass, 5 reeds, 4 fiddles and a ryhthm section of piano, banjo, sousaphone and percussion.

Established artists were eyeing jobs in the stage bands. Getting one was like a fresh plum. "Mutt" Hayes, saxophonist from Muncie Indiana, had left Ted Fiorito's Edgewater Beach Hotel Orchestra and joined Ash, feeling his Stage Band offered an opportunity for steadier work at higher pay. He was right. The hotels were experiencing darker days when diners didn't dance and dancers didn't dine, but they all went to the movie theatres. Several fellows who joined along with "Mutt" were to become leaders and M.Cs. in their own right - destined to do well in the large theatre.

Even with his knowledge of showmanship and his considerable natural talent, Paul Ash left nothing to chance. He was meticulously selective in the matter of musical craftsmanship. He could tell with one audition whether or not the guy or doll "had it" or would get "it." One of his best picks was a pretty gal from Evansville who was squired around by a husband with a noticeable limp. He became known as Colonel Gimp, and was so called by his friends as well as those not so friendly. But he was devoted and fiercely protective of his lovely wife. He would brook no comment about her shape, complexion, smile, teeth, or anything that did not speak of her voice and her song delivering ability. Let any wise-crack come from any direction - somebody had best wear headgear.

She appeared with Paul Ash during his most successful season, was featured many weeks, would move up to the Palace as well as London's Palladium along with Lou Holtz and Lupe Valez. She was tremendous in Mr. Ziegfeld's Follies. Her name was Ruth Etting.

Unfortunately Ruth Ettings don't come along like cherry blossoms in spring, and Paul Ash couldn't get by without a considerable sprinkling of established talent. He needed some ready-made class to recharge his batteries and booked some biggies now and then while moulding beginners into names to consider. Ben Blue, Buck & Bubbles, Lewis and Moore as well as Sylvia Froos can thank Paul for pushing them up the ladder. Sophie Tucker, Belle Baker and Jimmy Durante with his two partners can thank him for upping their salaries double and sometimes triple.

Paul made his Chicago employers, Balaban and Katz, a ton of money and he knew it. They knew it, and he knew they knew it. They especially appreciated Paul's value at Christmas when they sent him an envelope with a thousand dollar bill in it. Paul returned it marked "opened by mistake," and was unaccountably ill for a couple of days. When he received another envelope containing a $5,000.00 check - miracle of miracles, he made the first afternoon show.

Dwight Jones could scarcely control his enthusiasm, relating the bits and pieces of the Paul Ash story. "What a

Band! what arrangements! If you want to hear a tune really played, go to the Mc Vickers and hear that band." Dwight's pitch had its strongest impact on Dave Coulter. He had listened attentively, completely absorbed, and amazed everyone with a quick suggestion.

"Send somebody up there and take a look. I'll pay the shot. See if the idea could be tailored to the Ohio."

All present thought it would be best that Charlie go for a look-see and make any decisions, as he would have the ultimate responsibility for the success of the venture. He and Mir were on the Chicago Limited in nothing flat and soon they sat 6th row center in the Mc Vickers hearing and watching the "Great one" do his stuff. Watching more than hearing.

Paul Ash was featuring Sophie Tucker's son who aspired to emulate his famous mother and become a singing star. The poor lad couldn't sing, couldn't dance and wasn't too "handsome;" but with Paul Ash by his side, smiling appreciatively and drinking in every note the kid got out, even if off key, the guys and dolls in the first six rows loved it and gave out with applause like the boy was Al Jolson.

Mir Davis remarked, "There's the key to Ash's success. Just watch how absorbed he is with the fellow's effort, and how he seems to transfer that interest to the audience. It's like going 'uhm, uhm, uhm' eating spinach with the kids watching.

"Paul's great," Charlie agreed, "but he's got plenty of help. How's about those 19 guys on that bandstand. They know what this thing's all about. Don't you think?"

"I think you got troubles," Mir piped up.

"No troubles," Charlie thought and went into a haze wondering how and where to find a guy that touched all the bases to become a stage bandsman.

He not only must be a thoroughly schooled musician - a good sight reader and a competent technician able to follow a baton, he must also be familiar with the art of make-up and those inventions of Max Factor and his ilk. (Most of the lads were dubious about the benefits of grease paint, and would be happy to learn about the flesh-colored chalk that could be sponged on the face and easily washed off after the performance.)

Equally important, he must have a knowledge of spotlight behavior. His manner must convince his audience he's playing a glorious tune, and his smile and slight hesitation at the finish must say, "Thank you, Ladies and Gentlemen."

The fellow must be an actor. He is always on stage. A comedian, working in front of the band might tell some very funny jokes - funny enough to have the lads rolling off the bandstand, when they heard them the first time. However, the bandsman needs his stock of smiles, chuckles, and careful attention to the performer regardless of how late in the week or how bad the jokes. Georgie Jessel always claimed, "These guys in the stage band can kill a comic. They'd listen and laugh like hell for the first show. Maybe they'd pay attention the second show...but not too much unless they had to watch for a cue. After the first day they'd sit there with a "dill-pickle" look, yawning, picking their noses, and making memos on their music sheets. Did they laugh? Christ no. They'd heard it. Naturally, the audience would look at them, wonder why they weren't laughing, and decide the joke wasn't worth laughing at.

After the show Charlie and Mir found a table at the College Inn and talked things over. The coffee wasn't too bad. They agreed the whole stage band idea was beautiful. The band would be no problem; Indiana had good musicians all over the lot, singers by the dozen, and plenty of good acts readily available. Charlie might even learn to be an adequate Master of Ceremonies. But to do it at the Ohio - how? Small stage, screen in the way. No bandstand. No scenery. No lights.

Dwight had it all figured out beforehand. He explained, "All we have to do is get Charlie Kuhn to build a thin penthouse to accept the picture screen which he could pull up like any other piece of scenery, getting it out of the way and giving us a clear stage. Then he could build us a bandstand on rollers which could be pushed downstage for band numbers and rolled back for accompaniments. He could build an elevator to hold the pit piano, and wind it up for piano features and solos.

"Get someone to paint some scenery, rent some costumes, add some lighting, hire a couple of tap dancers, a girl singer, maybe a funny fellow with a few jokes, teach Charlie how to introduce acts, and voila! We've got a goddam Stage Band Show just like Paul Ash.

Old faithful Charlie Kuhn became the man for all seasons - stage carpenter, electrician, grip, and property man. In addition, he was in charge of rolling the band downstage for featured numbers and pulling it back at the finish of the tune, allowing time for well-milked applause. It wasn't easy with 2600 pounds of flesh and bone adding weight, but well-greased rollers and a maze of ropes and pulleys simplified the operation. The business agent of the Stage Hands Union conveniently looked the other way.

In event of a piano feature, or when Hoagy or Doc was scheduled to solo in the spotlight, again Charlie was called. He would grind up the homemade elevator, do a split second grab at the switchboard and dim the lights ready for "My Blue Heaven" or "At Sundown." The fellow had to be two places at once. Impossible, but that's the way it was.

One of the novelty sets. It featured "Music as you like it" and came within a few hundred dollars of equalling the Circle's gross.

It was a great experience, going from country to country in costumes with the faint cachet of mothballs or mildew. The Charlie Davis Band turned up in Russia, Mexico, Spain, France, and even in the Army, Navy and Air Force. On one occasion the lads ventured to Holland, wearing wooden shoes for a one-time corns-on-the-foot week. Never again.

They produced one of their most ingenious presentations when they journeyed to South Africa. Earle Moss had conceived a glamorous arrangement of a tune called "Black Bottom," written about the new dance craze. The opening was an intriguing prelude of drum beating, with everyone in the band beating on some special drum, stick, or shell. Earle was a genius at thinking up strange effects, and this mysterious theme was his best effort to date.

The band was behind a scrim curtain, beautifully painted in jungle colors and shapes. The stage was lighted in a green haze. The whole setting, music, lights and scenery was a classic example of unity and coherence.

Davis had spent some time in preparation of his introduction. He thought it necessary to explain the tune, the dance it represented, and the various effects the arranger was trying to detail in musical terms.

The curtain rose for Saturday's opening performance. Charlie, garbed in regulation safari trappings, entered the spotlight smiling his "Ladies and Gentlemen," acknowledging the applause, bowing and explaining: "Today the band is presenting a musical essay based on the new dance sensation called 'the black bottom.' It is, no doubt, one of the main features in the popular George White "*Scandals*, and all the lads and ladies here at home are trying to learn to do 'the black bottom.'

"Of course, we all know the original Black Bottom came from Africa where the Negro came from..."

At this point some bastard in the back row bellowed a stage whisper, "By God, he's right!" And the audience roared. Davis turned red to white and from white to red and with every change of color the laughing grew louder. It was bedlam. Everybody was having fun except Charlie Davis. He went into a little dance he used once in awhile - the laughter grew. He tried to speak - no way. It has been rumored that the folks were still laughing some years later when they tore the theatre down.

On that day, however, the Ohio Theatre and its homemade stage show became the friendly theatre. People came to see what they'd do next. What difference whether the picture was a goodie or a stinker — let's go and have some fun. The shows improved with experience. The stage presentation business was a new thought in Indiana entertainment, and "wouldn't it be fortunate if one could turn to page 140 and read directions on how to keep it fresh?" Only there was no book. New and different once in a while was easy, but new and different every week was something else.

The background for the homemade stage shows. While not in a class with John Murray Anderson's things, folks liked them...and came back week after week.

The emphasis had to be on sight entertainment. Regardless of how it sounded, the audience must **see** it to be entertained. The use of ultraviolet light on flourescent paint caused considerable stir. Occasionally the band did a stunt they called "With Bottles." Each bandsman blew flutelike into his own bottle which had been tuned by a certain level of water; the higher the level - the higher the note. When his note in the tune was called for, he jumped up and tooted, only to sit down and give way to the next note. Phil Davis and Harry Wiliford got bellylaughs when they did a la-sol, la-sol sequence sitting next to each other. Their up-down, up-down blowing-at-the-same-time scene raised the laugh level several decibels, and when Phil missed the chair and went down on his butt, the house went wild.

Adjourning to the new Columbia Club after the last show at the Ohio, and playing a couple of hours for dancing, got to be a night-after-night chore. Even a fistful of money at the end of the week didn't quite compensate for the days a fellow was too tired to play golf. What good is money, anyway? A lad or two called it quits. Bill Herring left the band and took an easier job down in Cincy with Henry Thies, and Fritz Ciccone, the master of the tuba, joined a Chicago band.

Although the band seemed to please the Ohio audiences, always generous with their applause, there was yet some question about the vocalists. Ed and Ralph were long gone, having caused quite a stir on radio with their "Sisters of the Skillet." And with Cy Milders going back to Hamilton, Ohio, into the laundry business, the lads hired to sing the vocals left a great deal to be desired.

Charlie and Fritz were all ears when they heard about a young fellow from Little Rock, singing with Dick Kent's group down at the Kentucky Hotel in Louisville. The scuttlebutt had it that Kent's band was running out of engagements and would break up. It happened, and Fritz quickly sent Dick Powell a paper to sign plus a ticket to Indianapolis. The kid was great. His range was even higher than Morton Downey's and his low notes had a quality that would tame the meanest Shakespearean shrew. His first vocal was "I Can't Give You Anything But Love, Baby," and as far as anyone knows, they're still applauding. For the first and only time ever in the band's experience, a singer sang an encore of the same song. The audience demanded it out loud.

Dick Powell had only the sketchiest knowledge of instrumental music, but he had a burning desire to learn banjo, trumpet as well as saxophone. At the close of his third week with the band he could play all the chords on the banjo, got rid of the rubber strings, took his place on the bandstand with the other instrumentalists, and joined Local #3.

Charlie worried a lot about Dick's hands. His gestures were godawful. He was finally told to do a semi-lean on the piano, or hold his banjo, or just try to stand relaxed and not move his hands. The spotlight man was instructed to light his head and shoulders only.

Young Powell's stage presence improved with every performance. The folks loved him. The kids thought he was the greatest, and the flappers screamed and squealed when he hit

Charlie Davis predicted a successful future for Dick Powell the moment he heard the boy from Little Rock sing his first song. He upped his assessment after noting Dick's ambition and willingness to pay his dues.

Charlie resolved to place little dependence on the lad, realizing Indianapolis would be only a stopgap in his climb.

The lad from Little Rock with the voice.

a high-note finish. Fritz was not surprised when Dick told him he and Doc Stultz had fixed up a ten minute act they'd like to try in vaudeville if they could get some bookings. A tough blow for the band. Charlie yelled his head off - "Here we get this guy, show him where Washington Street is, get him some decent food, and two months later he's gone, leaving a hole in the band as big as a gravel pit."

Things were moving fast and furious in the field of entertainment. Rumblings from Chicago brought Paul Ash back into focus. The Chicago entrepreneurs, Barney Balaban and Sam Katz sensed the old Mc Vickers wasn't the place for Paul Ash. It wasn't large enough, it was too run down, and it wasn't fair to his shows, classy as they were, to put them on in such a rag-tag pile of bricks. They therefore built him a beautiful new pile of bricks in the center of Chicago's loop. The Oriental had everything — a large stage, excellent acoustics, a feeling of intimacy, adequate scenery, and a talented group of stage mechanics who could build anything. Mir and Charlie saw one of Paul's shows staged in sort of a Taj Mahal interior with huge pillars on either side of the stage. When the show went into its finale, the pillars let down, forming stairways with beautiful, scantily clad showgirls, plumed and powdered, gracefully descending to the terrific applause of the audience. Mr. Ziegfeld would have been pleased, even if sore at Paul for stealing his stuff.

Chicago had lots of company in the many large movie palaces abuilding. Everybody and his brother in Indianapolis praised the Moroccan facade of the new Indiana as it took shape. It was going to be a beautiful building, 3500 seats, a huge stage, with a dramatic proscenium arch and everything to entice the paying customer. It was musician gossip that the new theatre would have a 50-piece symphony orchestra with Nathaniel Finston, the top Paramount Director, coming to open with Overture 1812.

The Circle theatre crowd had outdone themselves. The Liebers, Robert and Herman, A.L. Block of L. Strauss Co., Fred Gardner, Theodore Stempfel, and Rubush & Hunter were not only civic minded developers but forward thinking fellows whose taste of success at the Circle suggested an encore.

Herman Lieber and Mr. Block seldom missed a show at the Ohio. Block had just sold Charlie a fine raccoon coat at half price to use in the "Joe College" number, and Fred Gardner always stopped backstage with a little liquid present when the boys did a request he liked. Very nice, the band agreed, from fellows who never disdained a profit.

Charlie thought the new theatre was going to be a honey, but where in the hell were they going to get enough fiddles? It was during the week that organist Lester Huff and Charlie played excerpts from "Rhapsody in Blue" that Herman Lieber called.

Herman might not have been the ring leader if the Circle-Indiana group, but he held the respect of the other members. They had the utmost confidence in his judgement. They took for granted the clout he had with his brother Robert who was President of First National Pictures — a man with tremendous influence in the motion picture world. They were willing that Herman should be a one-man steering committee when it came to policy in the new theatre.

"Charlie," he said, "thanks for coming over. I wanted to talk to you about the Indiana. I like what I think I see. I think you are flexible."

INDIANA
A Great Theatre, Named in honor of A Great State

"Thank you, sir," said Charlie, with a questioning look.

Mr. Lieber had a lot to say. "It is my judgement the day of the large symphony orchestra in our theatres is passing. Even now, Barney Balaban, Sam Katz, Robert Lieber, and Buffalo's Mike Shea are toying with the idea of creating live entertainment units in the Paul Ash mode to travel a circuit of the larger theatres. New York Paramount's Boros Morros agrees. He's been busy forming a creative producing group - writers, composers, and arrangers. He landed Vincente Minelli as his scenic designer. It looks very much like the idea is jelling."

Mr. Lieber was certain the Circuit would include the Indiana here in Indianapolis and would require a stage band with a leader who would act as Master of Ceremonies. "Do you think you could gather 18-20 young musicians and mold them into a big-time stage band? Play for ballet as well as for tap dancers? With a drummer who could catch kicks and splits? Dream up a weekly band number that would be interesting? Build a following of loyal rooters like you had at the Ohio?"

"Mr. Lieber," Charlie thought for a moment and answered, "we could certainly try. Our band goes to Lake Manitau for the summer, but that won't keep us from putting together the band you want. We'll have it ready by the middle of September."

The summer at Manitau was strangely different from others. The old Colonial across the lake had been rebuilt, redecorated and reopened. It was beautiful, with a dance floor extending out over the water. The Colonial had engaged a knockout band from Cincy. Murray Horton's Orchestra had talented musicians, excellent arrangements, and good entertainers.

Charlie Davis' Band faced solid competition. The season at the outset looked like a season of tough going. However, with the luck of the Irish, the loyal following built up over the years remained loyal and many of the wanderers came back after a few visits across the lake. The season was not a record breaker, but it was above average, and it had some positive aspects.

The Horton Band at season's end had no immediate booking. They had nothing they considered a good prospect. But they did have a fantastic drummer.

Ralph Lillard had long been the top percussionist of the State of Indiana. He could do it all: drum, play tympani, bells, xylophone and marimba as well as compose and arrange. Fritz made him an offer. Ralph agreed to join our band with an *if*: If the Davis outfit would also give a contract to his friend, Phil Davis, the Horton trombonist - he'd join.

Talk about killing two birds with one rock! Fritz badly needed another trombone to fill out the five-brass in the stage combination. He had Phil's name on a contract in nothing flat.

Another piece of good news. Luck seemed to be coming in bunches. Fritz got a wire from Dick Powell asking if the band would like him back. Would a gray squirrel like some roasted goobers? And then Reagan Carey wrote a letter saying he was available. That would be great - Reagan back. With Karl VandeWalle, Reagan, and Ray Schonfeld the band would have a saxophone section as sharp as a tack. And more good luck: Earle Moss wired Fritz he would join and do the band's arrangements, play third trumpet, and fourth saxophone when he got loose from his present job.

A couple more fiddles, a bass, and a piano player and the band would be ready for the down beat. Labor Day found rehearsals starting - none too soon. Herman Lieber had it figured right: The Publix Units were on the way. He had heard from Boros Morros announcing the first Unit production - complete and opening in New Haven in early September.

"You can never sometimes tell."

    J. Russell Robinsom, seated at the Dixieland piano, presently basking in the aura of his "Margie" to the tune of $40,000 in early royalties came up with an idea. Russ thought Charlie Davis, writer of the sensational "Copenhagen" teamed up with himself as writer of the jazz classic "Eccentric" could produce a best selling tune.
    Not so. Their effort, a hotsy-totsy tune they named "Fallin' Down" got nowhere.
    While....

Fred Rose and Charlie Davis, who hardly knew each other, wrote a thing in about five minutes, called it "Jimtown Blues" and hit the jackpot that would pay royalties for 50 years.

6
velvet pants

Whether it was genius, careful research, or just dumb luck, the resourceful Paul Ash won his bet. His "new twist" had succeeded in making quick believers of the greats who ran the movie theatre industry. These gentlemen saw an opportunity to bolster the sagging grosses brought down by the poorer grade "A" pictures and most of the "B" pictures that came out of Hollywood every hour, on the hour, hour after hour. Their first act as believers had blossomed into the glamorous new Oriental, a monument to Paul's idea. It wasn't long before the weekly *Variety* published some unbelievable figures. The Oriental, without the super-class pictures, on many occasions outdrew the prestigious Chicago with all the big film names.

More and more top-flight exhibitors saw great potential in this new type of band entertainment and joined with Balaban and Katz to help form the circuit Mr. Lieber had envisioned. They found many cities ready and waiting, New Haven, Boston, New York, Philadelphia, Cleveland, Detroit, Indianapolis, Chicago and St. Louis had 4,000 seat palaces that would welcome this now proven box office success. The big wheels in St. Louis, Charlie and Spyros Skouras, who operated the Ambassador and the Missouri, even leased the Indiana and Circle to solidify their position.

To assure well-produced Units, a separate production company came into being, adopting the name Publix.

Publix recruited great producing talent: Jack Partington of light opera fame; John Murray Anderson, who had done excellent things for Florenz Ziegfeld; Jack Donahue, the crack dancer and producer of dancing routines, and Albertina Rasch, the coach-choreographer who organized fabulous lines of dancing girls as well as beautiful ballet units. For the superb orchestral arrangements, Adolph Deutsch, Victor Young and Phil Boutelje were drafted. The William Morris Agency provided a galaxy of top-notch ex-vaudeville performers and combed the nightclubs for young talent.

The first Publix Unit opened in New Haven, Conn., in midsummer, 1927. It had the distinct flavor of "old Italia" with Tostelli's "Serenade" and "Santa Maria" sung by an excellent soprano, Dorothy Neville, who was studying voice and hoping to enter Opera. A Rasch ballet group did a "Tarantella." Beautifully costumed, expertly lighted, their precision faultless, these girls left their audience breathless. Phil Boutelje had composed a finale especially for the Unit called "O Madre Mia," a striking melody that the Charlie Davis Band would use for a theme for years. With the glamorous Miss Neville singing, the cast on stage for curtain call, the lighting simulating falling blossoms, the effect of "Orange Blossoms" was one to remember.

When "Orange Blossoms" arrived at the new Indiana Theatre, Charlie and his boys were the stage band. They learned to fill those requirements Herman Lieber had specified.

The lads rehearsed the Tarentella as if they had been playing Tarentellas for years. Neville loved the way they accompanied her. She called her rehearsal quits in five minutes. "Great, boys - beautiful! Do it just that way."

Certainly, the band had done its homework, but how Charlie would make out as M. C. remained to be seen. The boys noticed their leader somewhat chagrined, or if not chagrined, at least not in the best of spirits. He was struggling to get into the costume furnished while getting instructions he thought were kind of picky from that fellow with the lisp and hands on hips. The director eventually made Charlie come on stage sans BVDs as they would show through the tight-fitting, black velvet toreador pants he had to wear. Charlie yelled his head off - "The goddam things are scratchy."

Program
(Continued)

Publix Theatres presents
"ORANGE BLOSSOMS"

Devised and staged by Frank Cambria.
"For thee, my love, a wreath of Orange Blossoms,
More pure and waxen than the Lily,
Thy bridal wreath of God's creation—
Would that they shall bloom for ever and ever."

1. IN A GARDEN .... THE TRYSTING PLACE
    Toselli's "Serenade" .... Eugene Cibelli
    "Serenade," by DiCapua .... Dorothy Neville
    Assisted by the Flower Girls
2. A VENETIAN CARNIVAL
    "Tarantella" .... Danced by the girls of the Ensemble
    Clown Capers by "Toots"—Dances arranged by Senia Gluck
3. INDIANAPOLIS' FAVORITE
    ### CHARLIE DAVIS
    and his Augmented Stage Orchestra
    playing a Selection of Popular Hits
4. NEAPOLITAN FESTIVAL
    "Santa Lucia" .... Dorothy Neville
5. EARL AND BELL
    a. "La Spagnola"
    b. "Just the Same"
6. DEZSO RETTER
7. A FLORENTINE WEDDING
    "At the Temple of Love"
    Done in the style of Tiepolo, a painter of the Italian Renaissance
    (Baldwin Pianos Used)
    General Music Director, Nathaniel Finston

He only had to wear 'em for a week. The next show was back to normal. Sport coat, white buck shoes, gray flannels, and a band parade number where the lads did a collegiate marching stunt all around the theatre with most of the kids in the first seven rows following in lock-step. It was a slick idea but the boys developed many others, discarded some old ones, and found out some things they should have known all along. The paying customer, while willing to be loyal, expected the loyalty to be earned - earned by a diligent search for new material - different, interesting, and even fascinating.

Soon after came "Top Hat" featuring a little gal that wore a top hat well: Ginger Rogers came to the Indiana just after she'd won a Charleston contest somewhere down in the sun belt with her baby-doll pumps and schoolgirl soprano. She was lovely - couldn't help but be with a mother like Lela who kept a watchful eye on her every movement and guided her into the upper reaches of stardom.

Many members of the older generation, men as well as women, came to the theatre to hear Dick Powell. Dick thought his following was principally teenagers, but he was wrong. There was a large flock of seniors, probably mothers, who thought they'd like to mother him, and they bought tickets with such thoughts in mind. There was also a pocket of middle-aged men and women, about equally divided, who faithfully came every Wednesday night for no other reason than to hear Charlie Fach play his trombone solo. Others came to watch Phil Davis' antics. A gang of kids went crazy when Lew Terman did his "Broken bow" trick on the fiddle. Lew would undo the bow hairs and stick the fiddle between the bow stick and the strings, playing four part jazz to the rhythmic hand clapping of the entire audience. Herman Lieber was not disappointed in his hope that the Charlie Davis boys would develop a following. They were taking note of the antics of the pros the Publix units brought to the Indiana week after week. Phil and Harry practically took lessons from the young fellow that had 'em in stitches in a unit titled "The Classroom." Ray Bolger, booked into the Indiana two or three times, could upset a study period better - and funnier - than anyone extant. Each succeeding performance was funnier than the last.

Meanwhile, the Indiana marquee had undergone a subtle change. The third or fourth week of the Publix Units saw Charlie Davis in lights. Sometimes even the picture star's name was omitted. Word had come down from the top. "Sell the sizzle, not the steak." How they figured the band and its presentation was a sizzle left one to wonder, but evidently the big brass noted better results when advertising an "in person" attraction. And so the marquee was programmed to read CHARLIE DAVIS BAND ON STAGE instead of SENSATIONAL PICTURE ON SCREEN.

It was no great chore for the advertising fellows to change direction at a moment's notice. The Indiana Theatre boasted of the classiest advertising department any theatre could ask for.

The big boss, Bill Goldman, had that rare gift of hopping everybody up, making fellows produce beyond their capabilities, and sprouting genius where no genius was.

His staff, Cullen Espy and Sturdy Sturdivant, could take one of Mr. Goldman's ideas and come up with a campaign that could sell any and all shows that were booked into the Indiana. Their promotional advertising and inviting marquee displays often turned a so-so show into a success, and a good show into a smash. Cullen Espy, an A1 lobbyist, could always guarantee a good review. Many a reviewer found it well-nigh impossible to write any sour rhetoric after one of Jos Starr's juicy porterhouse steaks and a sip or two of Weller's 107 proof Kentucky Sour Mash.

Sturdy Sturdivent was a past master in his field. He could dream up a promotion, get it on paper, explain to the artist exactly what he wanted and come up with a selling ad that put people in the seats. His knack was uncanny. It's no wonder the brothers Skouras took him away from the Indiana and sent him to the spots in their circuit that needed a trouble-shooter. Jim Long took his place and did a good job.

The band seemed to be making waves. Several of the Paramount big shots peeked in occasionally to watch the lads work. The Teetor boys from over at Hagerstown who ran the Perfect Circle Piston Ring Company had been catching the Band on occasion and thought it would be great if Charlie and the Boys would do a weekly radio program for their company. Robert Vahey Brown, WLW's star announcer, who later did the sensational "Breakfast Show" from WBBM, came over to Indianapolis to do the announcing. The Band broadcast from the Atheneum Ballroom, not the best acoustically, but good enough to send the program over the air to the sponsor's entire satisfaction. They employed the Band for the entire season.

Evidently the big guns at Vocalian Records heard one of the Radio Shows and suggested the band make a few sides for them on their next trip East. Charlie's lads were happy to have an opportunity to forgive and forget the dismal effort at recording some years back when they'd gone to Richmond unprepared. The Indiana publicity department had a real "chocolate drop" .."CHARLIE DAVIS BAND GOING TO NEW YORK TO MAKE RECORDS." The folks would eat that one up. They would come in droves to hear the famous band - now making records - now the biggest of the big! The pub lads pulled out all the stops. They arranged a parade, fixed it with Mayor L. Art Slack to make Charlie Davis Mayor for a day, and arranged a special advertising campaign, upping the budget 1,000%.

Charlie made Mayor of Indianapolis for a day

And then the roof fell in!

The Vocalian people got in a hurry and over-anxious, sending a recording team with a truckload of equipment to Indianapolis where they proposed to record the Band in the ballroom of the Atheneum, saving a lot of trouble and time for them. They wanted to get the Charlie Davis Band while it was hot.
But what about *"going to New York to make records?"*
The publicity department decided to change nothing. They'd brazen it out.

The Band cut "You're a Real Sweetheart," with Dick Powell singing the vocal; "When," with a vocal by Harry Wiliford and a trumpet solo by Charlie; "The Drag," a hot tune composed by percussionist Ralph Lillard; "Just Like A Melody Out of the Sky," with Harry's vocal; "Suppose Nobody Cared," a tune Charlie wrote, with Dick doing the vocal, and a couple of others that were not pressed.

Vocalion lost no time getting them on the shelves. They were on sale in time for the band's 1000th performance at the Indiana. The *Star,* the *News,* and the *Times* all carried news items along with the sizable ads announcing the new records. Charlie's tune got a good plug and the 1000th performance set a house record.

Hear "SUPPOSE NOBODY CARED" featured by CHARLIE DAVIS and his band in 1,000th Performance Show INDIANA THEATRE — "Suppose Nobody Cared" Vocalion By DICK POWELL — WEEK OF MAY 12th — Charlie's own number sung and recorded by Dick Powell

Not a bad song. It did nothing.

Ralph Lillard should have a complete biography in this book — a commentary on his abilities as a percussionist, his genius in "fitting in" a group such as *That Band From Indiana,* and considerable mention detailing his character as a gentleman. Ralph was the Band's favorite all around good guy.

The parade came off without a hitch. A few of the townsfolk thought it was carrying things a bit too far to hold up noonday traffic for a goddam band, but by and large the folks took it in good fun. Mayor Slack was most gracious. He was a nice guy anyhow. He proclaimed the day a *day for music and singing and keep happy - it's fun.* Certainly it did the town no harm to join in the spirit of the day. When the records went on sale, the counters were busy, the record dealers were pleased with the shot in the arm, and everyone thought the band recorded well.

But one of the reporters on the *News* who had never missed an Indiana show wondered, "How the hell did these guys go to New York to make records when they never missed a performance at the Indiana?" Two and two together never added up to 5. He smelled something, and it wasn't geraniums as he set about writing a piece about an affair that looked suspiciously like a hoax.

The accidental hoax.

The reporter wrote like he had a scared pen, hurrying to get it to his editor. Bill Goldman got wind of it and phoned the paper's advertising chief, gently reminding him of the ton of lineage he places in the paper. The story wasn't exactly killed - editors would never think of supressing news. They looked down their noses with total disdain at mere advertising hucksters pleading, "leave this one out."

Nobody ever found out what a hassle went on behind the scenes at the newspaper. No doubt there was bloodshed, but somehow or other the spicy story of trickery in the entertainment field, describing in detail the way the unsuspecting public is hoodwinked, beautifully written in a column of 1,000 words, got boiled down to a 1 column 2" bit down at the bottom of page 7 next to a small ad about Fletcher's Castoria.

Helen Boop-boop-a-doop Kane started the boop-boop-a-doop craze ... starred in a Jerome Kern Musical "Good Boy" and played the circuit to full houses. She was the Charlie Davis Band's #1 rooter.

- 65 -

Love Her? Why, the Town is Simply Wild About
HELEN KANE
Now "boop-boop-a-dooping"
IN PERSON at the INDIANA
If you never see another show the rest of your life, we beg of you, don't miss this one!

"BOOP-DOOP-A-DOOP" CONTEST TONIGHT!
See the Helen Kane-Indianapolis Times "Boop-Eoop-a-Doop" contest at the second stage show tonight! The five winners of Saturday night's preliminary singing to see who is Miss Kane's best "double" in Indianapolis!

---

big! big! big!

INDIANA

She's the New Sweetheart of Indiana!
Helen KANE IN PERSON
boop-boop-a-dooping with
CHARLIE DAVIS
in his big stage show
On The Screen
"HOLIDAY"
Year's mightiest drama with
ANN HARDING
Star of "Condemned"
MARY ASTOR
ENDORSEMENT
"Our finest show of the entire year."
Management

25 / 35 TO 1 PM

CIRCLE

Everybody's Cuckoo—But Oh, What Fun!
BERT **WHEELER**
ROBT **WOOLSEY**
master marvels of fun and laffter in
"The CUCKOOS"
Juggernaut of glorious joy with
JOBYNA HOWLAND
and 1,000 Others
All Seats 50¢ after 6 P.M.

25 / 15 TO 1 PM

OHIO Buddy **GIRLS!—** He's Here TODAY **ROGERS** in **SAFETY IN NUMBERS**

EXTRA! **UP THE CONGO**

Publix Units were becoming accredited successes, if not sensations. Big names sprinkled here and there together with big time productions and big stars of Radio and the New York stage sent grosses skyward. Helen Kane, the boop-boop-a-doop show-stopper from "Good Boy" broke the Indiana house record with $56,000.00. Some take at 65 cents top!

But it wasn't the high-salaried outsiders that did the trick. There were others, sometimes conveniently unnoticed, who had sold a ticket here and there. One kid in particular developed a sizable following. The guys would never forget Harry Wiliford, his trumpet playing, his singing, his flair for comedy. Where was there a more gifted triple-threat performer? Harry had more natural talent than any of the band members realized. He could mug a laugh out of an audience without knowing how he did it. He could fabricate a joke sequence by blurting out whatever came into his head. He could get belly-laughs by just walking down stage to a trumpet solo and then preempt further laughs by playing a beautiful, simple melody that would make one shed a tear. Such change of pace, such natural timing--Harry had it in baskets. Nobody knew where he got the pathos — pathos that wasn't his bag at all; but pathos he could reach back for, whenever he needed it. One could hear a bobby-pin drop as he sang, and the burst of applause at the finish was bright sunshine from dark night, all caused by Harry's ability to hold listeners in the palm of his hand and keep them there until he saw fit to release them with a grin.

"I'll get by as long as I have you."

Nobody ever did "Mississippi Mud" that great number of the late twenties that's supposed to have **made** Bing Crosby, any better than Harry. The great Crosby found that out when Paul Whiteman brought his large group to the Indiana with Bing

- 67 -

soloing the "Mud". Of course, we must make allowances for Harry's home field but the customers demanded aloud that he also do the number. It was no contest. No discredit to Bing, but Harry was the greatest—at least when we speak of "Mississippi Mud."

At another time he could take his trumpet down stage after playing a solo and sing to it, "As Long As I Have You." And Beautifully.

Luckily, Charlie Skouras didn't take the same view of Harry's ability that the boys in the band did. When he wanted someone to take over the Master of Ceremonies chore at the Circle Theatre he noticed no one but Dick Powell. Mr. Skouras thought Dick singing "My Blue Heaven," "At Sundown," and "I Can't Give You Anything But Love" put a lot of people in the seats. The Skourases decided to give Dick a band and a show of his own. They were certain he would help the Circle's sagging Boxoffice.

But who would fill Dick's shoes at the Indiana? One doesn't find fellows like Dick in the Sears catalogue. Audition after audition did not find a replacement. A few lads could sing melodies well, but no one could tell what they were singing about. Some did both melody and lyrics perfectly, but, gad! to look at them! They'd have to sing in a blackout. One fellow could sing like a lark - looked like a million dollars, but his ells came out w's. Imagine: "My Bwue Heaven" or "I wuve you." Then Louie turned up.

Fresh from Purdue University Law School, a clear tenor with perfect pitch he delivered a lyric sincerely, convincing the listener of his belief in the song's message. This ability, coupled with a good row of teeth, a boyish grin, and a shock of curly black hair helped the teen-age cuties forget their lost idol, Dick Powell. Audiences at the Indiana received Louie's numbers with warmth; their applause was especially enthusiastic when he sang his favorite, "I'm Just A Vagabond Lover." All the young kids wanted to hear that tune. "Where can we get the sheet music?" "What about records?"

Louie explained, "Boys and girls, you can't get copies or records anywhere. It's not published. It's just a little ol' ditty that's been kicking around Purdue for ages...we don't even know who wrote it."

But there's a sniff in the air. A sleeper? A song-hit sleeper. A sure-fire piece of music that would make some real money. The boys never got over the "Dreamy Melody" affair up at

Wauwausee when some fellows picked up a stray tune, put some lyrics to it, and sold it for a ton of money. "Vagabond Lover" looks like finders-keepers.

Who wrote it? Harry said, "I'll tell you who wrote it..ol' Joe Anonymous..you remember good ol' Joe? We just might be in a beautiful position to make this tune a biggie." They all thought it would be a good way to pick up a stray dollar or two, having had a peek at Charlie's last royalty check from "Copenhagen" - something over $2,400.00.

Charlie piped up, "Lads it ain't that easy. There's a lot of monkeying around before you get a tune on the music stands. You gotta write a verse, a piano score, simplify the range, and then get some publisher to sink some dough in it. It takes time and trouble. Count me out--this is the golf season."

The Circle had been booking travelling attractions. Big name bands, some small ones, some solid hits like the "Rhythm Kings" with Bing Crosby, Rinker and Barris. Among the groups were the Yale Collegians. This outfit had evidently heard Louie do the "Vagabond Lover," for a couple of weeks after they left, Charlie received a letter asking for the words and a lead sheet to the tune. The letter was signed in a scrawl.

"Fritz, who the hell is Rudy Vallee?"

After many experiments the lads came up with this one. Probably the most successful of the spot faces.

INDIANA

JOIN THE THRONGS that will acclaim Charlie Davis today and all this week

Today's the Day! The Big Show! The show you've been waiting for! Hey, Hey! A revel of jazz, joy and jollity. Charlie's gonna say "Thank you." C'mon! Let's go! Let's help Charlie celebrate!

CHARLIE DAVIS BIRTHDAY PARTY

Oh, Boy! New York acts! Peppy girls! Gorgeous scenic and novelty effects! It's Charlie's present to Indianapolis and he guarantees you the greatest ever!

and on the Screen
"A GIRL IN EVERY PORT"
With Louise Brooks and Victor McLaglen, Star of "What Price Glory"

This one did business.

INDIANA 35¢ TO 1 PM

LAST 3 DAYS!
CHARLIE DAVIS PRESENTS
PAT ROONEY
and Pat the Third
IN PERSON
Other Big Acts

Zane Grey's Mightiest!
JACK HOLT in
"BORDER LEGION"
Coming Friday
CLARA BOW
Two Big Stage Shows

CIRCLE /SKOURAS/PUBLIX/

Only 3 Days More—
Don't Miss It!
'sweet mama"
baring the secrets of two-gun racketeers with
ALICE WHITE
DAVID MANNERS

25¢ TO 1 PM

C'mon Friday!
GARY COOPER
in
"THE MAN FROM WYOMING"

OHIO FAMILY PRICES

LAST 3 DAYS!
Marie **DRESSLER**
Polly **MORAN**
in "CAUGHT SHORT"
LAUREL & HARDY in "BELOW ZERO"
See It Today!

The ad featured the cool air conditioning in both theatres. Usually featured when the screen fare was weak.

7
nothing except everything happened

Things refused to happen in 1928 - exciting things, that is, and 1928 became the year of the calm, reminding one of a long stage wait.
The stock market took the interest of the band fellows as well as the public at large. Phil Davis matured into an advisor.
— He had a yen for Cities Service, having doubled a small investment in a couple of months, and he explained the mysteries of buying on margin which resulted in the entire musical group spending their waking hours watching the tape over at Thompson-Mc Kinnon's.
Dessa Byrd went on a strict diet. She was always cute-plump, but must have had trouble getting into some of her underthings and decided it was time. The diet was severe, consisting of three-decker sandwiches of bacon, tomato, lettuce, and sliced hard-boiled egg. Thank goodness for the lettuce.

Pete De Paolo was basking in the limelight, having won the National Championships of '27 Racing. He was always a loyal rooter for the band and gave the boys autographed photographs of himself in his winning car. He told about the wonders of the super-charger, which the boys couldn't tell from a worn-out alarm clock, but they oh-ed and ah-ed Pete's exhaustive expositions.

Frankie Parrish took Louie Lowe's place as the band singer starting, of course, on the rubber-stringed guitar as a seated bandsman. Frank had graduated from Butler and had built an impresssive following of college kids with his beautiful tenor voice. He liked the idea of using language as an entertainment feature, and his German pronunciation in a favorite "Dein ist mein Ganzen Hertz," coached by a local German Professor, pleased the folks at the Mannerchoor and the Atheneum.

Frank could hit a golf ball a mile, only nobody ever knew where it went; when he got on the tee, everybody ran and hid.

A long line of big names in the theatre played the Indiana. Week in and week out saw Ben Blue, Joe Penner, Cy Landry, Ray Bolger or George Givot light up the marquee. Herb Williams played a week after closing his smash hit, "The Farmer Takes A Wife." Folks still remember Johnny Perkins twirling a lemon while preaching the qualities of the pineapple. He claimed the pineapple was the greatest brain food ever, and when Charlie noted, "That's not a pineapple, that's a lemon," Johnny said, "See, you're gettin' smart already!" And when Charlie asked Josephine Davis (she changed her name to Joan), "Did you ever hear the story of the traveling salesman?" She would answer, "I was the farmer's daughter." Whether the audience laughed for five minutes or not it was great fun.

Some of the recent stage favorites were attempting ill-advised comebacks. Eva Tanguay with her undulating strut and "I don't care" attitude, and Sophie Tucker belting out "Some of these Days" did their best to bring the past back into focus. Amber lighting, beautiful costuming, and the genius of the make-up artist couldn't do it. Charlie, who had idolized them before their twilight, wished they had quit while they were ahead.

The competition among stage bands was fierce. With leaders like Mark Fisher and Frankie Masters in Chicago, both excellent songsters, Mark having been featured vocalist with Ted Fiorito's Band at the Edgewater Beach Hotel, and Frankie always in demand for spot singing - the Granada and Tivoli box offices were busy. Eddie Lowry and Brooke Johns, both seasoned performers in the big time, ran the St. Louis shows to the satisfaction of the Skouras Brothers. Russ Morgan with his terrific trombone made a great name for himself doing the Publix shows in Cleveland. So the Davis band continued to seek out novelties that would spice up their part of the stage shows. The "bottleband" to the tune of "Wishing" got laughs and appreciative applause; a stunt with tin lids done in a well-rehearsed routine demanded an encore; the boys did an excellent job as a glee club when they sang "Ol' Man Noah" - after spending some weeks training with Jack Broderick's dance studio in learning a tap routine, they performed it in the theatre and it was a sensation.

Each week someone from the Indiana production staff traveled to Cleveland to catch the Russ Morgan Band presenting the unit which the Indiana would play the following week. He would then meet with the local master-minds to plan the antics that would enhance the presentation.

Milton Feld, Publix Vice-President, had good things to say about the Indiana operation. "You fellows put a Unit on as it's supposed to be put on. Your stuff always fits right in with the acts, giving the whole performance unity and coherence." The fellows thought he sounded like an English teacher, but they always remembered the compliment. It just might have been one of the reasons Publix invited Charlie to do four weeks of the 1929 season as M.C. at Broadway's New York Paramount - they kept him two months.

The New York Paramount house band was a good one. First chair sax and clarinet was a young fellow named Benny Goodman. Everyone predicted he would go places. Over in the brass section another comer, a good looking wiry trombone player the lads called Glen, who had a beautiful tone, just the right vibrato and a good row of teeth, would soon have his own band - "Glen Gray's Casa Loma."

It was nice to hear George Dewey Washington again. He'd been a favorite in Publix circles ever since Paul Ash had introduced him to Chicago a couple of years back. His "Keep Smiling at Trouble" was a classic and a lesson in philosophy to boot. The semi-cakewalk exit with top hat waving murdered the audience with a show stopper that demanded an encore. When the show couldn't move, he finally gave another chorus that brought Bob Weitman backstage to give Charlie hell for letting the show run overtime. Bob invariably apologized, saying, "There's gotta be a little son-of-a-bitch in every successful manager."

George Givot could do a "Knute Rockne" and completely fool anybody that ever went to Notre Dame.

"Wanna Buy a Duck?" Joe Penner was probably the best liked comedian that ever played the circuit. A very funny fellow...people loved him.

Herb Williams fresh from his success in "The Farmer Takes a Wife" was a sensation.

The "Champion," Pete De Paolo, was a great "fan" of the band. Caught every show. Never failed to request "Minnie the Moocher" with Harry singing it. He could answer Harry's Ho-di-hos from fifth row center and be heard above the rest of the audience.

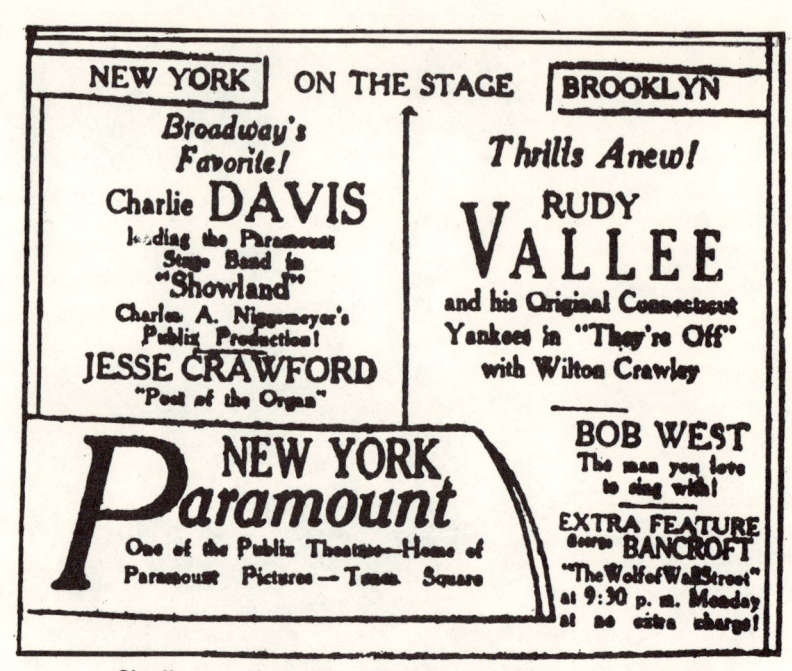

```
┌─────────────────────────────────────────────────┐
│  ┌──────────┐              ┌──────────┐         │
│  │ NEW YORK │ ON THE STAGE │ BROOKLYN │         │
│  └──────────┘              └──────────┘         │
│    Broadway's                 Thrills Anew!     │
│    Favorite!                                    │
│   Charlie DAVIS                 RUDY            │
│                                VALLEE           │
│  leading the Paramount                          │
│    Stage Band in           and his Original     │
│    "Showland"              Connecticut          │
│  Charles A. Niggemeyer's   Yankees in           │
│   Publix Production!       "They're Off"        │
│   JESSE CRAWFORD           with Wilton Crawley  │
│   "Poet of the Organ"                           │
│                              BOB WEST           │
│      NEW YORK              The man you love     │
│     Paramount                 to sing with!     │
│                            EXTRA FEATURE        │
│  One of the Publix         George BANCROFT      │
│  Theatres—Home of          "The Wolf of         │
│  Paramount Pictures—        Wall Street"        │
│  Times Square              at 9:30 p.m. Monday  │
│                            at no extra charge!  │
└─────────────────────────────────────────────────┘
```

Charlie never felt quite at home conducting the Paramount Orchestra. The men were excellent musicians but inexperienced in the fun and games side of the stage band business. He missed the lads from Indiana.

New York was lovely in October '29. People in residence in the big city never knew how lucky they were: no earthquakes, no tidal waves, no flooded rivers, no swarms of locusts. Just good shows opening, fine food in dozens of places, stores with everything one's child bride could desire, and a cool 67 degrees on the thermometer. But things were to happen to take the sap out of the city as well as the whole world: All the little guys who loved Cities Service; all the big fellows who were spread thin trying to make a killing; all the little old ladies who wanted to live a little bit better, advised by the nicest broker, to nibble a bit on some sure-fire investments — the whole kit and kaboodle were devastated. It was Black Friday.

Talk around the theatre was in whispers: too bad Bill Goldman was wiped out! Georgie Bishoff jumped out the sixth floor window! The damn market seemed to have no bottom. Gossip had it that Paul Ash saved Sam. Nobody knew for sure what the rumor meant, and each had his own version. Maybe Publix President Sam Katz had too much on margin and was about to be sold out when Paul, who had money like haystacks, came up with enough to patch up Sam's deficits. It was days before the Paramount audiences turned the corner toward normal. When a number finished, people just sat on their hands. However, time has a way of healing — widows don't wear black forever. The Publix gang out at Astoria redoubled their efforts, coming up with a hit Unit that featured Ray Bolger in his best comedy routine to date. Albertina choreographed a stunning precision kick routine for her line of 36 girls that had the audience cheering midway in their downstage movement - audiences at the Paramount seldom cheered; there was usually some suspicion connected with such activity. New acts were known to invite a few friends to sit in various parts of the theatre, to stir up a cheer or two coupled with heavy applause. Paramount's manager, Weitman, who made a specialty of evaluating an act's quality, took a dim view of any semblance of a claque, and Mrs. Rasch would have no part of any unforseen cheering, but she was delighted when this line of her beauties stirred the house.

When Charlie came back from New York the band tried something new. The boys dressed collegiate in red sweaters, white trousers, and white buck shoes. They had special stools made about eighteen inches high and painted white. While Charlie was announcing the number, the boys would line up downstage except for Jack Drummond who would stand with his string bass, and, of course, Kenny Knott would remain at the piano. All the others would be in line on their stools. Even Ralph Lillard, drums and all, would get downstage in nothing flat. It was an exciting move and often got applause. The band would then do about 20 minutes of memorized arrangements, solos, and a line-up for the glee club number.

It didn't take long for this change in atmosphere to catch on. It must be that people like hustle and bustle, or maybe they like to see fellows working, especially musicians who are supposed to be sedentary even if they play lively music. If the quick change from the bandstand to downstage - everyone lugging an instrument, even drums and bass fiddle, plus their stools — was a source of considerable glee for the audience, they knew only the half of it. Each week while doing four shows a day with five on Saturday and Sunday, the band had to prepare a specialty for the next week - not only prepare, but memorize it. It would be like cribbing for an exam to read music, but the notes had to be invented, scored, and extracted. Charlie Davis had the greatest arranger in North America—Earle Moss, who doubled on subordinate trumpet and tripled on fourth saxophone when needed. Earle could score about 400 bars of 19-line music, if given a modicum of quiet and four pots of steaming black coffee, and still play thirty shows a week, if the coffee didn't throw him.

Because of prohibition, coffee had to do, for a stronger substitute—at five dollars a pint—was not in the budget. But there appeared on the scene—not an angel of mercy, not a modern Sir Galahad—but a modest corner druggist. Mr. Barnhardt, a gifted pharmacologist and schooled chemist — was lucky to have around, and timely, as he invented a flavoring agent that mixed with some water and ordinary grain alcohol, was not too bad a restorative, and certainly did not approach the price the robber barons were getting for bonded whiskey. Mr. Barnhardt's secret formula was never to see the light of day, though guesses were rampant— juniper, lemon oil, bitter almond, a mystery herb that nobody could place. The classic drinkers suggested the taste was reminiscent of the better washed gins of the glorious yesterdays.

Having discovered the beneficence of Barnhardt's mix, plus 14 ounces of good grain alchy and six ounces of water drawn from the tap, Earle found he could get through a couple of nights in his newly sheetrocked arranging room and tickle the lads with the unusual showstoppers he'd connive and transfer to paper. His buddy Reagan Carey, would be there ready to extract the score, make individual parts, and have here and there a sip of Mr. Barnhardt's.

"Who" from "Sunny" won accolades from the bandsmen, the ushers, the management, and half the town, judging from the way the audience whooped and whistled when the band played it. It was Moss' finest hour. His arrangement was inspired.

Earle did forty weeks of those arrangements. The band committed forty to memory, and Charlie collected forty weeks of traffic tickets for parking his Packard roadster in the alley back of the theatre: the sign "No Parking, Police Order" was clearly visible, but the police were all nice guys and the blues that took care of the block around the theatre came in often to catch the show backstage - anyway, Charlie didn't think the cops were in earnest.

In fact, Charlie didn't think.

—— INDIANAPOLIS SESQUICENTENNIAL EDITION,

SUNDAY, NOV. 7, 1971 ——

DAVIS IN 1928   DAVIS IN RECENT PHOTO

(Charlie Davis, popular Indianapolis bandleader who won a national reputation in the 1920s and 1930s and whose band featured Dick Powell, has written for the Sesquicentennial Edition a humorous account of how his 1928 arrest for parking tickets led to a stage skit, a contempt of court charge and an amusing "battle" in court. Davis now lives at Oswego, N.Y.)

Parking Tickets Really Entertaining

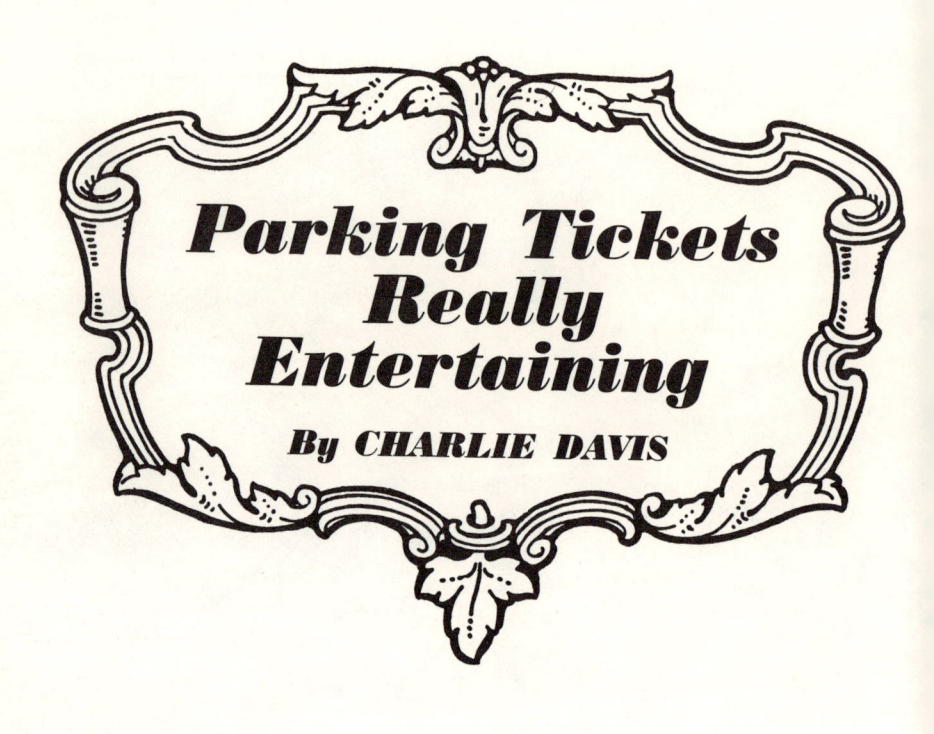

By CHARLIE DAVIS

It was the 362d parking ticket that broke the spell.

A new police wagon stopped behind the Indiana Theater where we were playing and the officer in charge asked, "You got a fellow here named Davis?"

Our good friend the stage doorman tried to outwait the policeman but finally answered, "What's Charlie done — murdered somebody?"

"NO, HE JUST disobeys the law four times weekdays and five times on Sunday, when he parks his car on this spot. See that sign 'No Parking Police Order?'"

The ride across town was a little bumpy and the siren made it a little noisy as it terminated at the jail-house, quite different in appearance from our better hotels, but looking fire-proof and safe.

I was not required to register; a man registered for me. I made a mental note that the iron bars would have a neater appearance if, as in the larger banks, they would be of brass or at least brass-plated.

Four reporters listened closely as some man asked me if I wanted bail and, "How do I plead," and so on. The officer in charge, one of the reporters and I had one thing in common . . . we all three had the same bootlegger.

I phoned my wife who immediately flew off in all directions saying, "This is my first encounter with a jail-bird. You just stay put 'til you hear from me." What else does a guy do in jail but stay put?

HOWEVER, I soon was released and advised that Judge Cameron's court would take up my matter in the morning and that my wife had arranged for Attorney John Ruckelshaus Sr. to represent me.

This arrangement delighted me; with the thought of the outstanding forensic talent of John Ruckelshaus dignifying a case in traffic court, the drama began building. Mr. Ruckelshaus was a great lawyer. He reminded me of William Jennings Bryan, whom I had the good fortune to hear back in '15 when he spoke at one of the Wednesday Assembly periods at old Shortridge High School.

In comparing the two, several points of parallel strike one quite clearly: they both had that reverent tear in their voice when mentioning our country; they both reduced their delivery to a whisper when speaking of the flag and they both climaxed with head-shaking, jowl-rattling vigour when they intoned DEMOCRACY.

With this feeling of well-being I traveled over town just in time for the second show at the Indiana. Evidently the news of my arrest had spread. Laughs and titters welcomed my entrance on the stage.

OUR BAND number that week once again showed the genius of our arranger in our special treatment of a great tune called "Mississippi Mud" with the vocal chorus by Harry (Dizzy) Wiliford.

Harry had mastered the finesse of singing this type song as it should be sung. Even though Paul Whiteman the previous week had featured the Rhythm Boys with Bing Crosby doing the number, when Harry did it one felt, "That's the song — right there — that's the song."

No doubt the audience felt the same way, as they stopped the show everytime Harry performed. And when I say stopped the show I mean exactly that — I couldn't move that show for as long as twenty minutes on occasions.

The evening News hit the stands with a good sized headline:

"DAVIS FINED SIX HUNDRED, SIXTY DOLLARS"

That morning I had paid the fine with quite some relief because the judge had set the penalty for my transgressions, regular price at $5 a ticket which would add up to $1,810.

HOW RUCKELSHAUS did it I'll never know, but as he pointed to the flag, "If the court please," he said. "We all love that flag and we all respect it. We all live under that flag and we are grateful for the blessings we receive while living thereunder. The honorable judge, when he sits on that bench is wrapped in that flag as he metes out the justice due every American. And he is a fair and honorable judge."

And thereupon the figure fluttered down to $660. I just happened to have my checkbook with me.

I have often wished we had left the entire matter in the courtroom, but no — we could not miss the opportunity to capitalize on this embarrassment and its attendant publicity. Therefore we set about our writing.

"THE STORY OF A DAY IN THE COURTROOM"

Stage setting: Background, curtain in No. 2
Properties:
   Judge's Bench —(stage center)
   Table for attorneys (right stage facing)
Cast of Characters:

Murderer	Harry Wiliford
Arsonist	Phil Davis
Attorneys	Fritz Morris
	Ralph Lillard
Traffic Violator	Regan Carey
Bailiff	Earle Moss
Judge	Charlie Davis

Scene No. 1 "ARSON"

Bailiff brings in arsonist
Attorney appears
Attorney:
   And so you've been a-burning things
      A Matcher, you're for hire?
   The law views dim your specialty,
      Your should refrain from fire.
Judge:
   And as we find you guilty
      And catch you in our trap
   We warn you of the penalty
      And give your wrist a slap!
Attorneys, judge and prisoner shake hands and prisoner exists.

Scene No. 2 "MURDER"

Baliff brings in murderer.

Attorney appears
Attorney:
   You're here before this honoured court
      You're charged with Murder One?
   I tell you now in certain terms
      That something must be done.

Judge:
> Sir, go out and sin no more
> > And your book will close
> But if you ever kill again
> > We'll punch you in the nose.

Attorneys, judge and prisoner shake hands, slap each other on the back, exit.

Scene No. 3 "TRAFFIC VIOLATOR"

Bailiff and several g u a r d s bring in accused in Chains (wait on 2-minute laugh)

Attorney, assistant, secretary and council all appear.

Judge:
> Have you got $660?

(wait for laugh . . . keeps building . . . do not move)

Judge:
> You're a mighty naughty person
> > You should hang your head in shame!
> If people flaunt and laugh at law
> > You'd be the one to blame.

Attorneys: (suggesting compromise)
> Why don't we get our heads together
> > And give you our report?
> You then pass the sentence
> > that's the duty of this court.

Bailiff, roughing up the defendent causing quite a commotion finally quieted when Judge raps for order. All face the Judge to hear sentence:

Judge:
> Call the barber,
> > Shave his Hair
> Send him to—

> > THE ELECTRIC CHAIR.

BLACKOUT

Well, the audience had more fun, more giggles and more plain, clean enjoyment from this piece than anything I can remember having done. We actually meant no disrespect to the court in offering this light lampoon, but Judge Cameron took an entirely different view.

Allowing us the courtesy of a full week's performance, the man with the paper came after the last show Saturday night. "Contempt of court."

I called Ruckelshaus quick!

And so, at 10 o'clock Monday morning, the theater manager, the advertising manager, a representative of Skouras-Publix (our owners) the actors involved in the skit and myself presented themselves in Judge Cameron's court.

The judge read the law, down-graded the lampoonry, decrying the total effect such fun-poking would tend to have on the operations of justice in America, and further stated that whatever punishment could be considered maximum, would be the penalty.

I had visions of a long winter's and hot summer's stay somewhere without air-conditioning or equal convenience when John Ruckelshaus began.

"May it please the court, I know of the deep hurt these lads in their frivolity have caused you to endure. I further know of the inestimable damage they well may have done this honorable court by their absence of thought, but I beg to inform you, kind sir, that no malice was in their thinking — and harm to you was not their desire."

And again with deep reverence pointing to the Flag:

"But you know and I know that we all love that Flag, and we all respect that Flag, and we are all grateful for the blessings . . . that Flag . . . that Flag . . ."

Case dismissed.

And then another letter, signed in that same scrawl: Rudy Vallee had included "The Vagabond Lover" in his Heigh-ho broadcasts. He had knocked off some of the raw edges, made it more commercial, given it a verse, and sandbagged the Leo Feist Company into publishing it. "The Vagabond Lover" swept the country at the speed of light. Teenagers everywhere requested it; sheet music sales counted in the thousands, and Rudy's Victor record led the popularity race. His image and the Vagabond Lover became one and the same — he made a picture under that title. Royalties poured in: everything was roses until a character from out west was heard from. The fellow didn't seem like a songwriter, and certainly not a poet, but he claimed authorship of "The Vagabond Lover," produced a Library of Congress registration plus a copyright, properly dated, and demanded recourse. It was pretty hard for Rudy to believe such a cowboy could breathe the sensitive lyric into this song, and he had his doubts that the son-of-a-bitch could even whistle it, but he wanted no hassle and gave the fellow the greater share of the $1500 advance money for a quitclaim.

He never saw that guy again, but soon found out that the skirmish just settled had been nothing but a preliminary. A well-dressed fellow from Chicago introduced himself as C. C. Brown, Attorney at Law, opened a cordovan briefcase, and carefully brought out some well-notarized papers. Rudy's lawyer studied the documents with considerable care and saw uncontestable and utterly genuine proof that this counsellor Brown from Chicago was the composer, lyricist, and sole owner of "I'm Just A Vagabond Lover."

An S.O.S. was blipped to Charlie Davis.

Rudy was desperate, pulling out all the stops, determined to unearth any and all discords that might crop into the matter. Charlie Davis couldn't help him one way or the other. Everyone in Indianapolis knew that Rudy hadn't written the tune, so Charlie sent him a wire, "I can't help you. I'd better not get involved."

Rudy gave C. C. Brown a sizable split of the royalties and a promise of future checks and sent him back to Chicago with a pocket full of money. The residue to Rudy amounted to four or five thousand, but combining this with the lovelies the tune added to his fan clubs throughout the country, the profit rendered by the "Vagabond Lover" was considerable.

Give some credit to Counsellor Brown who conceived the beautiful melody and lyrics.

Give some to Rudy who squired it into the lyrical mainstream of the tune-filled twenties.

Give some to Louie Lowe and to That Band from Indiana who discovered it asleep and caused its awakening.

HEIGH HO, EVERYBODY!

Rudy liked the Charlie Davis Band ever since he heard the lads at the old Severin Hotel. He heard the "Vagabond Lover" as Louie Lowe sang it. Asked for a copy and was promptly ignored. Everybody was sorry.

The accompanying picture was taken by a passerby. The iron, barbed wire fence protects some kind of rock adjacent to Yale University. Already M & C quit saying ain't.

Miriam and Charlie would never forget the incident they called "The Big Hassle." The mini-upheaval came about when Paramount-Publix dreamed up the wild idea of juggling their MCs to different theatres in the circuit. The company thought a new face in the program would stimulate business, and that Charlie with his considerable expertise could teach the several bands to do a better job in unit backup.

Miriam said no. No Traveling. Tell Boros Morros to go and fly a kite. We stay put right here in Indy and that is that. But was that the way it was? Charlie thought the Paramount people probably knew what they were doing and should be given some kind of cooperation.

After a period of violent agitation, the upshot had Charlie making like a wild goose and doing the MCing trip as requested, with Miriam staying put in Indy, planning her garden and immersing herself in keeping the H.F.B. But sometimes upshots don't shoot according to plan. When the big C.C.C.& St. L. made the four minute stop to pick up passengers, Miriam B. was sighted rounding the corner with two bags and a raccoon coat. She was the first one on the platform, puffing like a calliope. Charlie told her she'd ought to quit cigarettes.

8
look, look, the marquee

The marquee wasn't kidding — they were all there: Dave Rubinoff and the pit band, the acts, the dancing girls, and Duke Ellington's Band in formal dress. The lighted billing topping them all belonged to the carpetbaggers, Charlie Davis and his Joy Gang. Whoever invented the Joy Gang soubriquet was never found hiding under the table, but it didn't matter too much; the boys could live with it. They were happy to be there — Joy Gangs, carpetbaggers, or whatevers.

The projectionist had come from the receiving room with eight cans of "The Royal Family" under his arm. He was getting a spirited going over from Dave Rubinoff. Folks wondered what it was all about. "You don't haf to spot my brudder," the great one complained. Evidently yesterday's spotlight had wandered wide, leaking over into the second fiddle section, with brother Hymie basking in undue illumination.

The Duke and Charlie were engaged in a spirited discussion about jazz music. When he found out the composer of "Copenhagen" was this Charlie Davis, the Duke couldn't get over it. "Great piece--great," he said over and over, complimenting George Johnson's sax chorus and Bix's cornet break. He predicted Bix especially would be heard from--and soon. Charlie was surprised at some of the maestro's comments. Duke didn't think jazz was a matter of color or locale; didn't think it had to be a rewrite of the composer's original inspiration, but thought the effect could be wrapped in a neat package without distortions of slurs and slides. His band played well-written, well-rehearsed arrangements, and he brooked no extemporaneous variations. The effect was cleancut precision, balanced voices, and an easy flow from *fff* to a whisper without any dip in intonation or tonal quality.

The rehearsal was a breeze, not different from the many rehearsals at the Indiana. The new show featured no other big names; Duke Ellington was the main attraction and probably used up most of the budget. After 15 minutes the band was ready, and everybody was home free for a couple of hours. Charlie and Mir Davis decided to test out an eating place they'd heard was the finest of the fine. Over on Forsythe Street, where the ghetto meets the Manhattan bridge, Manny Wolf's lived up to its scuttlebutt. The proprietor, Mr. Wolf himself, greeted them warmly and pointed to the picture of Charlie he'd just hung on the wall, joining the many celebrities of stage and screen. The luncheon pleased them immensely, and the Davises told Mr. Wolf they'd be back between shows. He invited them to have a pony or two of his Courvoisier cognac that had just dodged the revenuers and found its way to Forsythe Street, but Miriam thanked him saying it seemed a little early, and suggested the promise of a raincheck. Prohibition was a masquerade in Brooklyn.

The peepholes in the curtain told the story of the audience - not a pushover, but one that could be had.

The first three rows were filled with teenagers, ready and willing to meet new faces, hear new tunes, and applaud new singers. Already the Band from Indiana saw the nucleus of a following. Each fellow picked a prospective lovely who just might be on his wavelength. Charlie gave considerable thought to whether he should open with "Ladies and Gentlemen" or a "Howdy, Folks." He wondered if his own particular brand of Indiana corn would catch on in Brooklyn. He had no fear of speaking to an audience of the intelligentsia, but then, statistically, all movie-goers are twelve years old, so he settled for "corn."

```
NEW YORK                                              BROOKLYN
              Paramount
                    IN PERSON!    FREDRIC MARCH
                        TED       INA  CLAIRE
                       Lewis
                       High Hat      "ROYAL" FAMILY
                  Tragedian of Song      OF BROADWAY
                With His Musical Klowns
  BACHELOR FOUR    CHARLES WITTIER
  ELENORE BROOKS  and 36 Thrilling Girls
                                                On the Stage
                   - On the Screen -      The Three Greatest Bands
        "THE                              Brooklyn Has Ever Heard!
     GANG BUSTER"                         1. DUKE ELLINGTON
                                             and his Cotton Club Orchestra
     JACK OAKIE                           2. CHARLIE DAVIS
                                             and His Music Makers
      "Illustrations"
                                          3. RUBINOFF
     JESSE CRAWFORD
```

The Charlie Davis name was in the ad...about the same size type as the biggies. The band was in good company.

The curtain went up to scattered applause. Rubinoff had warmed the audience with "Orpheus," adding the organ to the finale. Folks could hear it clear out to Coney Island so undoubtedly those seated in the theatre, if not stirred, were at least awake. Maurice, the featured organist, picked a good one for his solo. With the screen's jumping balls pinpointing the words syllable by syllable, the folks sang themselves hoarse as they belted out "Show Me The Way To Go Home." It might have been sung better, but never any louder.

And then the Duke and his orchestra took over.

After their first number it was no contest--the band had 'em eatin' out of its several hands. "It Don't Mean A Thing if You Ain't Got that Swing" made everybody want to join with the jive, and "Mood Indigo" played to a humming audience. After a couple of encores and a sincere thank you by the Duke, the curtain closed for a short news reel while the band left the stage and the unit presentation took over.

The regular unit length had been shortened somewhat for the Ellington showing, but the acts were good. The Diamond

Brothers did their "falling plank" trick that scared everybody to death, but the comedy routine that followed put the folks back together again. A sister team looked beautiful and sang well. Cy Landry, always a favorite, did some pantomime and a terrific dance that laid 'em in the aisles, and the *Four Chinese* executed their patented pyramid stunt that always was a showstopper. It was remarkable, the sense of balance these fellows had, and uncanny how they juggled dishes, bottles, and even knives, throwing them at each other with never a cut or bruise.

The band's turn came next. To *that band from Indiana,* given the next-to-impossible chore of replacing the fabulous Rudy Vallee, it seemed as if the powers that be were looking for a fall guy who could take the heat until a proper successor could be hired. Surely the customers wondered why Charlie Davis had been picked. They soon found out and were taken aback a bit when a swarm of red sweaters and white pants suddenly formed a line downstage, on little white stools, and awaited a downbeat while their director was mumbling something about being happy in Brooklyn and declaring nobody could replace Rudy, but the boys would give it their best.

Charlie knew how to pick 'em. He had the boys feature a half dozen tunes that Rudy had made favorites. Charlie Fach did a trombone chorus on "You're A Real Sweetheart" that was pure class. Frankie Parrish, in excellent voice, sang "The Best Things in Life Are Free" which caused the kids up front to stop the show cold by demanding an encore—but no way. The fiddle trio sawed out a Joe Venuti special that knocked 'em on their ears while the boys were getting set for "Who." No band before or since played this gem from "Sunny" like the Charlie Davis Band. The last chorus with its sustained trumpet flare had the audience standing and as the flares turned into screams, the place all but came apart.

It had long been the policy of the Brooklyn Theatre management to check audience reaction after the first performance of a new show. The ushers were instructed to circulate among the poeple, listen to comments, and summarize them on a report sheet. Charlie persuaded one of the kids to give him a copy:

CUSTOMER COMMENTS

Paramount NEW YORK • BROOKLYN

ushers - Ray Long 4:30 P.M.

First Show __1/25/31__ Date

OVERTURE	Dave Rubinoff	*good - Dave in fine form - finish inspiring*
ORGAN SOLO	Maurice	*Audience sang well on: "Show me the way to go Home"*
FEATURE PICTURE	" The Royal Family "	*fine picture - a classic*
SPECIAL FEATURE	Duke Ellington's Orchestra	*Excellent... especially "Mood Indigo"*
PUBLIX - UNIT	Charlie Davis and his Joy Gang	*Sensational*

Cloud nine wasn't high enough.

The first three rows of teenagers caught all four shows on opening day and went out spreading the word. The turnstiles clicked like Halloween ratchets. Such pushing and scrambling for tickets had not happened since Helen Kane's record week — the box office was tickled pink; the boys were pleased — they didn't have to do anything but rehearse the new acts for a few minutes and prepare their specialty which was a pipe. Earle's famous forty, already composed, arranged and memorized from the long stint at the Indiana, were ready for rerun. Kenny Knott remarked, "It's a shame to take the money." "Time on my Hands" was no longer a tune but a state of being. Harry Dizzy offered, "Like I say, we can always eat."

Then it was back to Manny Wolf's for dinner — he was ready for Charlie and his lady. In no time at all a waiter materialized with small tenderloin steak sandwiches, hash brown potatoes, and broccoli garnished with sour cream, lemon juice and dill. He opened a bottle of Rosé to complement the selections, not knowing it was Mrs. Davis' favorite — she was all smiles. After an unhurried spell of making like trenchermen, they welcomed the waiter's reappearance with a picturesque tortoni. Manny had the final say when he brought them ponies of Creme de Cacao (dark) floated with heavy cream. "No problem getting the Creme de Cacao, but just you try getting heavy cream in this man's town."

On the Brooklyn Paramount west elevation.

Brooklyn's Joy Ambassadors!
CHARLIE DAVIS
AND HIS MUSICAL BOYS!
a program that's sweet and hot !

"WESTWARD HO!"

Publix Stage Show!
featuring
Mrs. Riley's son George
Queen, Queen & Queen
Karlton Emmy and His Mad Wags
Gorgeous Marbert Girls!

St. Patrick's
Day Melodies!
RUBINOFF
and the Paramount
Orchestra!
ELSIE THOMPSON
at the Organ

Next week's ad - not bad

By rights the Davises should have had it. But Charlie loved to eat. While not a gourmet, gourmand, epicure, or whatever, he could distinguish between salt and pepper, had an incurable love for "sweet and sour," was a devotee of onions — all ages, sizes and shapes — and could relish Mexican Chili seven days a week, even for breakfast. He did not care if the tomato was a bastard cousin of the deadly nightshade, nor did he agree with the early students of animal husbandry that the potato was fit only for pigs.

Barney Gallant's was a good bet over in the village — not too far to walk, and Charlie had heard that a Notre Dame classmate was M.C. doing a cluster of songs and chatter. A small combo led by Julie Styne was in the middle of "Night and Day" when they were seated. Julie had lately arrived as a big-time composer with a good sounding band to boot.

Barney's Club probably took the MVP award for being the coziest and most intimate of the village clubs. Barney never forgot a name and this remarkable knack stood him well as even the most formidable social figures liked to be greeted in the stage whisper that could be heard in Jersey. "Good to see you again, Mrs. Harbishin-Verpath," as he personally ushered her party to a ringside table. And if all the ringsides were taken, the bus-boys would quickly bring in another, placing it just inside the ring in front of a party not considered quite as top-ranking. Nobody thought anything about it, however, and the second liners were happy to bask in Mrs. HV's glitter.

The Davises enjoyed Walter O'Keefe immensely. Walter seemed to be glad to see Charlie. It had been ten years. People forget after ten years, but with his total recall plus that County Kerry gift of making a fellow feel important, Walter didn't need a brush to spread it on just thick enough. He had made a vast improvement since his '21 days in the Notre Dame Glee Club when Charlie was his piano accompanist. Not only had his singing style jelled into a song-selling ability to render either comedy or serious subjects, but his delivery as Master of Ceremonies classed him as one of the real artists in that field.

It seemed good sense to stop by Julius'. Nobody ever thought of going home to bed without stopping by Julius's — one of the village's favorite spots featuring delicious clam broth, always nice and hot. How Big Joe got so much body in it was his well-guarded secret, and you could taste it all day and all night and never discover the trick of the sweet-salty pleasure you sipped along with a tall glass of the draft and a pretzel or two. This was indeed *joy in the simple life.* Everyone marvelled at the effect their decorator achieved in reproducing a venerable Down East pub. Catering to seafaring hearties who liked their "drop of the creeter" among the spider webs, sawdust, lanterns, whiskey barrels, and other artifacts, this place seemed to make a preliminary gin and vermouth something of an imbibing comfort.

It had been a full day and a replete night. The hotel mail slot held two letters, neither with an Indianapolis postmark. One was a note from the manager of the St. George Hotel offering a thirteen week contract to play after-theatre dance music at the hotel's Roof, the other an invitation to play a NVA Benefit performance a couple of weeks hence. Playing benefits seemed to be the going thing in the City. A band could play one every night in the week and two on Sunday. Everybody and his brother had his hand out. Being invited, however, carried a certain cachet of prestige. Nobody was invited unless he was considered Big Time.

What a day it had been. Charlie and Mir sang along with Pippa, "All's right with the world."

9

gettin' smart already

It was inevitable — sooner or later there had to be a show aboard ship — a naval vessel with the boys in the band dressed to the nine's in white duck, white shoes, and gob whitehats, with Charlie in charge as Lt. (J.G.) bearing lots of braid: the "flag-waver" had long been a surefire success in the field of American theatrical production. George M. Cohan had reaped well, both financially and aesthetically, singing to and about Old Glory. His "I'm A Yankee Doodle Dandy" gave him an image, and "Over There," a niche in ASCAP history.

The Brooklyn stage spared no expense in reproducing the deck of a destroyer. It was believable. Under the magentas and pale blues, the audience had the feeling that the encounter had been won and it was time for celebrating. The grand old Flag flew high with nary a rip nor a tear.

The Publix Unit was a fun thing. Cy Landry, who never failed to "get 'em giggling" from the moment of his stumbling appearance, did a gob dance he'd invented especially for the setting. The Albertina Rasch line of girls added a hornpipe routine of sorts, mixing tap and soft shoe emulsified with a couple of pirouettes that made for a complementary change of pace.

The featured number introduced Gertrude Niesen, a newcomer to the stage. Nineteen, handsome, loaded with poise, she worked to Charlie downstage — it was not a Sunday school lesson: Gertrude torched the controversial "Love For Sale." Red-faced Charlie on the receiving end didn't know whether to brazen it out or drop through the floor, but the folks loved what they saw and heard. The melody was beautifully sung, and the high-note finish brought the house down. The audience caught some of the lyrics and were happy about that, but if they missed some, who cared?

Gertie could catch 'em in a fog.

Gertrude Niesen was a solid hit — the girl would go places.

The Brass section played a quintet arrangement — a rather difficult transcription of "Sailing, Sailing, Over the Bounding Main." Earle Moss had invented an unusual sequence of barbershop harmonies that seemed to be pleasing but probably not worth the effort. It went over fairly well, if not a smash.

Then "Dizzy" Harry did "Minnie." It was the first time he tried "Minnie The Moocher," which was just beginning to catch on. The fact that she was a "low-down hoochy-coocher" caught the fancy of the teenagers if not the parents. Like it or not, however, there wasn't much the old folks could do about it. The tune was a great novelty with its "hi-de-ho" answer bit that encouraged everyone to get into the act. Harry sang it for the first time without blowing a line:

"I'll tell you the story of Minnie the Moocher.
She was a lowdown hoochy-coocher.
Whatever Minnie did, she did it well,
An' every guy in town was under her spell.

Harry:	Ho-de-ho-de-ho
Band:	Ho-de-ho-de-ho
Harry:	Ho-de-hi-de-hi
Band:	Ho-de-hi-de-hi

and on and on, kicking it back and forth. Harry gave out with the second verse, but when he hit the chorus, he had company — lots of company. His first "Ho-de-ho-de-ho" was answered by the band with scattered help from the first three rows. On the second "Ho-de-hi-de-hi" about half the theatre joined in, and at the finish about three thousand people gave Minnie the loudest tribute ever accorded a lowdown hoochy-coocher.

The folks came to be entertained, and entertained they were. Harry felt good about it. The theatre manager claimed he never saw such spontaneous audience participation. Whether or not Minnie belonged in a naval scene was never given a thought. The number was moved to the next-to-close spot after the first show.

The finale didn't need to wave the flag — it *was* the flag, a battle at sea with the brilliance of exploding shells. The band whooped it up with an *fff* chorus of "Anchors Aweigh" followed by a repeat in stop time, the chorus tapping out the stops and then making a direct segue to their famous chorus-line kick routine. What a thrill to see a gem of choreography prefectly executed by sixteen lovely girls, all the same size, all kicking measured height in perfect unison, backed up with thrilling music and kaleidoscopical lights.

It was a difficult show for the band. The boys thought, only three more days - then the weekend and out of the sailor suits.

The Ted Lewis Band was booked for the coming week, and the Joy Gang would have it easy. Ted romanced a top hat and gold-headed walking stick about as well as anyone who ever walked into a spotlight. With his patented strut and "Is everybody happy?" getting a concert of affirmatives, he needed little else to create his classic image. He was a showman's showman, selling his song, his band, and himself and everyone was buying. Ted was a master of song delivery; his "Me and My Shadow" was unforgettable. The listener was hard put to hold back a tear as he strolled down the avenue, followed by his shadows, wondering what life is, anyway. A great gift, this ability to turn on emotions. Lewis' "When My Baby Smiles With Me" was honed to masterpiece sharpness. Everything was there: the twirling stick, the picturesque strut, the top hat tricks, and his exciting voice. It all dramatized his lean-back, half cakewalk, hat-waving exit..."See yuh later, folks!"

"Is everybody happy?"

When muh baby smiles at me

Dressing rooms were at a premium at the Paramount, but Charlie was thrilled to be asked to share his with Ted. The arrangement worked out fine. A down-to-earth fellow from Chilicothe Ohio was certainly welcome in a Hoosier's dressing room, and Ted Lewis at once became number one in Charlie's book. His wife Miriam seconded the motion after a small incident that happened midweek.

It seemed that Mrs. Davis had come to the theatre strictly out of funds, as was her situation generally. She had a project in mind—a project she had probably dreamed up within the last half hour. When she was out of funds, she customarily called her husband on the telephone and gave him a story, sometimes upholstered with spur of the moment thises and thats. But she was not near a telephone; therefore, she came to the dressing room — only to find Charlie gone for a haircut.

Finding her husband somewhere else, her jaw dropped almost down to here, with a look of despair reserved for those who are walking the last mile — a look that did not go unnoticed by the genial Mr. Lewis. "It can't be that bad, Miss. Maybe I can help?"

"I wanted to find Charlie — to give me some money," Mir said, smiling in abject apology.

Ted Lewis, in one quick motion, came out with a 50 dollar bill. "Here, maybe this will tide you over. Are you a friend of Charlie's?"

"Oh, Yes, I'm his wife."

"So much the better," said Ted.

The Paramount-Publix Unit producers learned the secret of the successful show by watching others. Members of the Astoria staff — the huge corps of writers, directors and arrangers, and even head honcho, Boros Morros — paid close attention to the Broadway goings-on. They never missed the Music Box with its several productions of "The Little Show," which boasted three great stars, Fred Allen, Libby Holman, and Clifton Webb, who established a never-miss format for a show the Astoria boys could apply to the Publix Units successfully viz: Hire a good singer or songstress, a good dancer, a funnyman; give 'em some good material, a good song or two and an occasional line of girls, and you're off and running. Jack Partington or John Murray Anderson would invent a setting or a novelty of stage craftsmanship, like Anderson's "Flying Pianos;" Phil Boutelje and Ruby Cowan could be counted on to come up with some pretty music and lyrics, and the rest of the Astoria gang would put it all together while Boros threw rocks at it. But when Boros was finally satisfied, they'd send it to New Haven for a warm up. If it were bad — change it; if good — send it to Boston, Brooklyn, and New York.

So that's the way they did it, and a star of the "Little Shows," Libby Holman, was coming to Brooklyn. Hopefully, she would sing "Body and Soul."

Meanwhile, the St. George Hotel offer had to be considered. The band had not played dance music since the days at the Columbia Club. Stage arrangements were a far cry from danceable music, and stock arrangements available were not written for sixteen piece bands. Still, it might not be bad to give it a try. Fritz and Charlie reasoned that the more people who heard the band, the higher it would climb.

The Joy Gang played at the St. George Roof six nights a week from 10:30 until 1:00 for dancing. When a tune came along with a soft baritone saxophone solo, accompanied by light-light rhythm; or when Fritz, Ralph Bonham and Art Berry gave it their best with the violins; or when the mutes were stuck in the brasses and Lillard used nothing but soft burshes, the couples would go into their cheek-to-cheek act with little or no movement and never want to quit, but when sixteen fellows lit into a stage hit with full brass and everyone blasting away, the folks wanted to run and hide. Fortunately, the band lads learned fast, and there were no casualties.

Libby Holman *did* sing "Body and Soul;" she also sang "Moanin' Low." Both songs were met with avalanches of applause. Libby's stage personality was warm and sincere, and her delivery was extremely convincing. She had that singular knack that made every man believe she was singing only to him. Remarkable — she was almost blind. Libby requested the stage hands chalkmark X'd circles indicating the safe area in which she could work, for she had a horror of falling into the orchestra pit. Charlie would often stagewhisper "Back, back" and wondered if the audience heard Libby's song over his whispers.

Wednesday of Miss Holman's week looked like a long day's night. The Joy Gang had to make a quick change to the St. George, play a couple of hours, and then *segue* back to the Paramount to play the first of the many benefits the Band would undertake. Reagan Carey recorded the incident in a journal that he kept.

> The Charlie Davis Band was scheduled to do a band specialty act on the NVA benefit show at the Brooklyn Paramount Theatre in early 1931. The show started after our last nightly show and lasted all night and far into the morning. We waited for our turn on the bandstand behind the curtain. All the big time acts were there; Eddie Cantor, Clayton, Jackson & Durante, East and Dumke, Berton and Mann, Ted Lewis, Eleanor Powell and many others. We waited, waited, and waited until about 3:00 A.M. at which time half the Band had fallen asleep.
>
> Suddenly the pit Band flew into "Clap Hands, Here Comes Charlie" and the curtains parted. We tried to awaken each other, grabbed our horns and stools and vaulted off the bandstand, enroute to the footlights. All did not go too well. Frankie Parrish tripped on the way down and spread-eagled onto the stage with his banjo spinning off toward the wings, Jack Drummond fell over his bass fiddle, Coofie forgot his horn, Ralph Lillard pulled out his drum platform and forgot to set the stage screw which let it go almost across the stage, three of us who made it to the footlights promptly fell off our stools.
>
> The audience loved it, and laughed and applauded — I think they thought it was a comedy act. We then managed to settle down and do our act, which went over very fine and we were very grateful after our unrehearsed comedy opening."

The Davis Band played 100,000 miles of George and Ira Gershwin without ever growing tired. Some things were certain: "Rhapsody in Blue" was one hell of a gem of country fiddlin', and "Girl Crazy" was a magnificent show. The Davis lads were delighted when Ginger Rogers, one of their favorites from the early Publix Unit days, made her smash in it. *Girl Crazy* was responsible for the introduction of yet another captivating freshman. A stunning slick chick with coal black hair, the reddest of lips, a figure to stir the fancies of springtime with a dynamo voice that blasted a song as no one before or since has equalled in natural timbre, Ethel Merman gave the band the treat of all time when she barged down stage and gave out with "I Got Rhythm." "And when I say 'gave out', I don't mean spoon-fed" Charlie declared. She belted out that great song in a manner to stop all discussion about who could belt the beltiest. No microphone, no electronic devices of amplification, just her own out-sized vocal chords that meant business and cast a jaundiced eye at the modern crutches and dealer helps needed by popular whisperers of the day's songs.

Although the Hoosiers were getting to know their way around in the big city, they were still feeling a bit like carpetbaggers, wondering whether the Indiana corn was showing. They approached the Merman early morning rehearsal with here and there a butterfly stomach, wondering how this gal, hot from Broadway, would assess a group of out-of-towners with instruments.

No cause for worry. Ethel was charming, saying simply, "Boys, follow me." "Probably the easiest job of following we ever had to do," Ralph Lillard announced. "All I had to do was thump out a downbeat and make like a metronome." One could feel the throb. Her downbeat was the same as Ralph's, and every upbeat had its extra accent. When she hit her second chorus of "Rhythm" she climaxed it by holding a high note for sixteen bars while waving her arms up and down as though she were flagging a train, her index fingers sticking straight out of her clenched fists, generating a ride like they hadn't heard since they left Illinois and Washington Street.

Merman wowed 'em in Brooklyn. The folks loved her; the boys in the band loved her, and, no doubt, the man in the box office loved her. At the finish of the week she told the Joy Gang how much she'd enjoyed working with them. Every man in the bunch wished her good luck and health in her career and said she couldn't miss in the theatre.

She commented, "Well, *Girl Crazy* did much for me. I was lucky, and maybe I'll get another show someday...who knows?"

* * * * * * * * * * * * * *

Quite a spell and considerable water over the dam since the little guy with the stunning blond visited Fairview Gardens on Lake Manitau in Rochester Indiana. The band fellows remembered him from the time they'd played behind potted palms at his family's de luxe shindig over in neighboring Peru. It had been a classy affair: gents with patent leather shoes and dames in long dresses carrying hollow-stemware filled to the brim with bubbles — prohibition was on the books, but only for people who didn't know any better. The Porters of Peru Indiana looked upon it as a pesky pox and everybody there had been vaccinated.

The little guy with the blond had brought the band a tune he said he made up himself. He asked the lads to try it. Not bad. A catchy melody and excellent lyrics about a boy and a girl on the back porch. Said his name was Cole...like the big circus people from Peru. The lad came over to Fairview many times that summer. He was going to Yale.

Cole Porter was a master of the inner rhyme:

I'm sure
if
sniff
Terrif-
ic'lly

high
guy
sky
my
i-
dea

"The Merm" sang it in *Anything Goes*. She got another show.

Fritz, Karl, Phil
Gene, Harry, Reagan
the "Floradora Sextette"

    Sustained ripples of laughter, always the end result of a performance by the band's Floradora Sextette—was most gratifying to the lads who perfected this unbelievable figment of their imaginations. Their grace, even if pseudo, was plausible. Their rhythm, maybe a bit herky-jerky, followed the downbeat of Victor Herbert's immortal "Heliotrope" ballet faithfully, notwithstanding some club-footedness, but fortunately without casualties.
    The credit line in this piece should go to Gene Woods who was the choreographer as well as the prima ballerina. The highlight was the "Showering of the Flowers," at which moment the members of the Sextette strew imaginary flowers at Phil, who gracefully acknowledged their courtesy. The whole thing was a study in prolonged belly laughs.

It would seem ridiculous to suspect a rash of homesickness infecting a group of men of voting age, living well, moderately successful in realizing their ambitions, not hurried or pressured by the passing of time, but remarks that were somewhat unbalanced had wormed their way into the daily chitchat-faint whispers of discontent that became a groundswell of rumblings. To be rational, one would suspect the fellows were simply feeling a letdown from their initial knockout success. Naturally, when things were simmering down and the customers came into the theatre knowing what to expect, they did not bend over backwards to make a big deal of it, nor did they wear themselves out applauding. The cracks that everyone agreed were widening in the otherwise cohesive unit appeared because the lads were maturing. They were thinking of families, schools for children, homes to be built and lived in, opportunities to develop skills to provide a living and eventual retirement. These were long range plans — not homesickness.

Fritz and Charlie also did their share of thinking. They knew that, sooner or later, each would have to go his separate way. Fritz would soon correspond with his Dental School pals, telling them to reserve a room for him one day. Charlie would count the months and days when his ten-year promissory note to his bride would come due. The Band was playing with the same verve and dispatch; the customers were loyal in keeping up their attendance; the management was pleased, and Milton Feld was glad he'd recommended the Band from Indiana; But the steam was escaping little by little.

One was never at a loss, while tramping the bricks of New York or Brooklyn, to find a stopping-off place where fun and games could be played, chewed or quaffed. Quaffing was the going thing in these days of restraint. Restraining was something done by those who didn't know any better, and a good quaffer was not hard to find. Charlie Davis and his lads, well employed in the daytime and early evening, were always and invariably searching for places of entertainment over and above the ones the man in the street found accessible. The lads had heard rumblings about a place of intrigue, a place close by, not to be entered by a knock on the door but by a most mysterious "Open, sesame!" combination of words that would make for admittance. Guys and their dolls entered, waited for the peep hole to open and announced, "Benny

Lapidus" in answer to the question, "Who sent yuh?" 'Twasn't easy, this admittance to the Latin Club, snuggled in behind Ebbet's Field, so close that a long home run would plow through the roof if the wind was right, but once one had passed through the iron doors he had, in one fell swoop, scored a social victory. He had made the grade. Nobody bowed and scraped. One was considered welcome — no more, no less — and ushered noncommitally to a table at some distance from that of the Borough President whose group included an assistant district attorney and a local magistrate, neither of whom ever expected Prohibition to set in. The gang was delighted with this "see no evil, speak no evil" headquarters of the big wheels of Brooklyn.

Betty Moss, who'd always wanted a taste of genuine Vodka, downed a jigger of it neatly. "It tastes just like Barnhart's Gin," she decided, and Earle lifted his cup to the grand old druggist back in Indianapolis who, he claimed, had prevented his mental collapse.

It would have been more pleasing if Charlie and Mir had been treated with some deference, for their guest of the evening was Eddie Cantor, certainly a person of considerable standing.

Eddie was the current attraction at the Brooklyn Paramount. Fresh from a round of personal appearances and Radio scripts, which kept him busily on the go, it wouldn't be a bad idea to relax, even for an hour or two. He worked pretty hard on stage. Doing his "Toot Toot Tootsie" accompanied by his famous skip and hand pitti-patting, with encore after encore, he always finished wringing wet. Mir thought Eddie would enjoy the delicious food and might like to review the impressive wine list as well as pick and choose the crisp delights of a salad bar second to none.

The Latin version of chicken cacciatore with the several pastas was strictly no contest, being far and away superior to any other in the immediate reaches. The flavorful capon, sliced, in tandem with the al dente elbows also defied comparison in the field of specialized comestibles. The feature of this particular visit, however, had nothing to do with food. Where it came from, nobody knew or would say, but this Club served a brandy (94 proof) that, when rolled around in the snifter, gave off a fog that could claim any award of superlative merit. It was said that a certain Col. James Balsch, prior to his departure on the *Bremen* laid in a case of the same, to assure himself of a decent drink, in case he chose to get barrelled in Paris.

Eddie wasn't hungry

But Eddie didn't drink, so no cocktails. Elaborate as it was, he seemed to have a struggle with the menu and wound up ordering some minestrone, a salad and not much else. Wishing he was back at 170, Charlie, at 185 pounds could no longer get into the velvet pants of "Orange Blossoms" — with or without B.V.D's — and he and Mir ordered the same as Eddie.

What had happened to the great man's toot-toot-tootsie effervescence? How come his pitti-patt had left the scene? Eddie Cantor was not the same black-faced showstopper known to the ticket-buying folks with the quick ten dollar bills. Some change had come over him; his conversation sank to a depth lower than forty fathoms. He never gave an inkling of what was wrong.

It was a chance meeting in the men's room which has that peculiar faculty of interpreting the grapevine, that clarified matters. "It's too bad about Eddie," Earle Moss commented. "He's been completely wiped out in the market... $86 G's worse than nothing." His Saturday paycheck would be the first on his way back up.

The news about Eddie had the boys in deep thought. A mental re-evaluation, contrasting Eddie Cantor's troubles with their own piddly discomforts, left them thinking things might not be so bad after all. If the lads had a siege of long faces, Rudy Vallee's visit turned them to Indiana smiles.

"You guys got it made," Rudy argued. "Everybody thinks you're great, and the management is delighted." He took Charlie aside and advised, "All you need is to get yourself better known — you gotta get a press agent." So Charlie hired a press agent, a fellow named David Green, who was reputed to be among the best, at a cost of $50.00 per week.. He immediately gave Charlie a beautiful 12 x 15 hard-bound press book with enough blank pages to accommodate 10,000 clippings.

Ten good pairs of legs

And the clippings started to come. A few samples should be sufficient to set the tenor of the campaign:

"Not long ago, Charlie was studying the music of the masters in the Latin quarter of Paris."

"The boys decided to give up Bach for Berlin and depart for Tin Pan Alley."

"Isham Jones' musicians left a trail of broken hearts among the chorines, but Charlie Davis ruled that his musicians leave the theatre the moment the show is finished and go to his hotel with him."

"Charlie Davis, popular M.C. at the Paramount once ran a scandal column... shame on him.

"Under the tutelage of Charlie Davis, famous Notre Dame halfback of 1921.."

Charlie commented, "I never saw the Latin quarter of Paris, never ran a scandal column, never saw the dames in the picture, and never even made the squad at Notre Dame. This stuff's a lot of garbage." Charlie collected clippings for about a month and then asked David Green to cease and desist as his $50.00 would not be forthcoming from that date.

INDIANA

PORTLAND, ME. EXPRESS
Star Of Radioland

Charlie Davis

Charlie Davis, former Notre Dame guard, is hitting the air now. None of Charlie's opponents on the football field ever suspected him of having music in his soul, but that's the way it is. Charlie is leading an orchestra which broadcasts from New York regularly over an NBC network.

NEW YORK AMERICA

ORCHESTRA TO TOUR

Charlie Davis, orchestra leader, is making a collection of the hit tunes of Broadway shows during the past ten years, and will present them in symphonic form during a vaudeville tour. The tour will take him as far south as Texas.

Heink will sing Bohm's "Still Wie Nacht" and the lovely cradle song of MacFadyen. Her string ensemble will play Mozart's "Turkish March" and the weirdly beautiful "Solvejg's Song" from Grieg's "Peer Gunt Suite."

CHICAGO, ILL. AMERICAN

Charlie Davis was a football star at Notre Dame, now he is maestro at the Hollywood.

NEWARK, N. J. STAR EAGLE

Charlie Davis, grid star, whose music is heard on WJZ at 11:00 P. M.

I NEVER HAD A CHANCE
Fox Trot
CHARLIE DAVIS and his ORCHESTRA
BANNER RECORD No. 33089

SO. BEND, IND. TRIBUNE 1934
SUCCEEDS.

—Central Press Photo.
CHARLIE DAVIS.

Charlie Davis, former Notre Dame guard, is hitting the air now. None of Charlie's opponents on the football field ever suspected him of having music in his soul, but that's the way it is. Charlie is leading an orchestra which broadcasts from New York regularly over the CBS network.

PHILADELPHIA, PA. RECORD

When Charlie Davis was a student at Notre Dame he played guard on one of the best teams that famous school turned out. He also took time, among his other activities, to direct the college orchestra. It was Hunk Anderson, noted gridiron coach, who persuaded Davis to take up orchestra work professionally when he was through at Notre Dame. For more than a year he appeared with his orchestra at the biggest motion picture theaters in New York. Then he went to the Hollywood Restaurant, from which his smooth rhythms now come over the air several times a week to NBC audiences.

Charlie Davis.

HACKENSACK, N. J. BERGEN RECORD
FOOTBALL TO MUSIC

Charlie Davis, whose dance band is heard over WEAF on Mondays at 6 p. m., took up music at the suggestion of Hunk Anderson, famous football coach.

DETROIT, MICH. NEWS
SHORT-WAVE BLUES

Charlie Davis, former Hoosier dance leader whose band is heard over WWJ from New York, is composing a new song, "Short Wave Blues"—his first attempt at composition since his famous "Copenhagen." The song, to be introduced shortly over NBC networks, will have excerpts of music representative of every country that can be reached on a short wave radio set.

Clippings, clippings and more clippings.

When the master minds of publicity suggested Charlie make like a chef, they didn't realize he would become a cooking addict. He never failed to try a new recipe, cooked up more disasters, and burnt more chocolate sauce than anyone known to date. But give the fellow some plus marks: He invented (or stole) a great recipe he called "Kaiser Paste." He concocted a melange -a vegetable affair with chicken flavor he named "ratatouille" although he couldn't pronounce it, and his trick of cutting leg o'lamb into round steaks and oven-frying them was something to rave about. He'd never become a cooking genius but he'd try.

Baton or ladle — take your pick.

Some guy in a gray flannel suit stopped by to talk about a short subject. He was from Warner Brothers and had an idea for a band feature based on some kind of musical journalism, to be shot in the setting built for "The Front Page." Everybody in the band had enjoyed the Ben Hecht-Charles MacArthur movie and started to think up stunts that would look well on camera.

And something else happened — the Band was being transferred to the New York Paramount for a stint. Broadway at last.

10
that flag!

Say what you want, make fun, let out strange noises if it suits you, but you gotta admit, there's only one Broadway. The big names are all there — the marquees a table of contents listing those who claim the popular fancy. A missing name tells the story of a star in discard, maybe for reshuffle, maybe forever. A name blazing in lights on Broadway is the accolade given to success; it is also the start of the finish.

Forty-third Street was something special — the Paramount Building, Walgreen's on the corner, the Astor Hotel with Child's Restaurant across the Street, theatres and hotels all over the place. Looking across, there was Loew's State with a new MGM picture; around the corner, the Rialto with a brand new Western; up the Street, the Palais Royale with Paul Whiteman's magnificent Orchestra. Guys and dolls standing on one foot and then the other, impatiently trying to get upstairs to dance to the maestro's "Whispering," had to be content with the melody filtering down from the bandstand.

Matinee music accompanying the color of the lights, big signs, bright lights, lights in daytime — who needs lights in daytime? The crowds, going where, coming back from where? All sizes of people, all colors, all forms of dress, hats, caps, berets, turbans, and bareheads. You name it. And that thing on the flatiron Times Building keeps flashing the news...flashing the news. The stage door, just a few paces from Walgreen's, invites you in. You wish someone would stick you with a pin. You can't realize what's going on, a crazy trick some dream is playing. The Paramount's massive pipe-organ is doing its thing: Jesse Crawford must be at the manuals. He didn't learn that instrument yesterday, and must have paid his dues a long time before he got to show off at the big theatre.

And then that feeling, a certain exaltation, much like the realization of victory against the odds; like the country ward heeler finally getting elected sheriff, or the mudcovered doughboy at last pinning on the Eagle of Lieut. Colonel. The cornfed Hoosier, looking up, getting the roof of his mouth sunburned, broke into his widest smile when he saw it. Out front, three stories up, was the Flag. Not the Stars and Stripes—a big blue Flag with white letters—big white letters:

CHARLIE DAVIS AND HIS JOY GANG

One's name on a flag over Broadway is like a kid explaining to his dad about his A+. What is A plus? "Dad, that's more'n you can get."

We who are in the business of huckstering music for dancing -- two-steps, waltzes, polkas, and the like, are finding it necessary from time to time, to seek out certain specifics which are acting as fortifying agents and are keeping up the level of verve and dispatch well nigh indispensable in such business. I am at once taken back to the bare-knuckles dispute over the relative beneficence of **Jasper Corn** versus **Tarboro Peach**, each straining to lead the field of elixirs having the greatest therapeutic value.

Tarboro, as you all know, is one of North Carolina's brown-bag cities giving a dance they are calling the **Spring German**, where they are inviting our band to play dancing music if we are getting into town and safely out of the same, which I am being told is not the easiest thing to do. From the very first instant we are hitting the town, we are getting to like a liquid substance they call **PEACH**, which has little or nothing to do with the fruit itself. Nor is it in any way suggestive of the graceful beauty of those bodies we are seeing walking up and down the main street of Tarboro, waving bright colored scarves and also waving other items of interest. **Peach**, itself, very likely is having some medicinal value which has been cut and somewhat diminished by the free esters they are never charcoaling out of the liquid. I, personally am not having the vaguest idea of what esters are having to do with the stuff anyway, but I am giving my advice: "Be wary of free Esthers, free Mabels or free dames of any ilk."

Even though we are finding some who are liking **tarboro peach** with a reverence known only in the circles of the most reverent, we are finding those who are passing it off with a shrug of the shoulder and a flip-flop of extended hands and are attempting to be saying come-see-come-sah.

Bacon and eggs tasted pretty good at Child's. Sunny-side up and basted, with no waiting, just the ticket — entirely satisfactory until one ventured up to 49th street and discovered Lindy's where the eggs were just as good but in addition one could look around the room and pick out here and there a legendary character. Over in one corner holding court was none other than Damon Runyon whose series of short stories in *Colliers* was the moment's sensation of the printed word. One could easily tell he was king of the hill, top of the heap, and patron

Jasper Corn is a horse of a different color, if we happen to be discussing horses at the given moment, which, of course, we are not, and, therefore, we are getting back on the track and investigating **Jasper Corn** in some depth. The revenuers are long a thorn or mayhap several thorns in the sides of the shotgun element in Indiana's hills who are hiding certain combinations of tinware and copper tubing and are performing such minor miracles of chemistry that are turning the juices of Silver Christmas or even Golden Queen into flammable liquid that is burning down the barn if left too long without the close attention of those gentlemen who are taking time to siphon off some of the top juices and are filling glass bottles which are holding about one quart and are turning into dollar bills as soon as they are finding stoop-shouldered fellows with hang-dog expressions.

Gentlemen, I am mentioning these matters to tell you of the dangers you are encountering in this easy flow of morals today. If and when some strange fellow is coming to your house, bearing gifts, as they say, these gifts being in the form of liquid something or other, and you are not noting a portfolio or some other item to distinguish an insurance salesman or a fellow selling a used car with one owner, the very minute this gent is bringing out a bottle and he is reciting some new kind of poetry in which he is extolling some virtue or other virtues of such full bottle, please be taking the advice of this friend, and see that you are checking the label if and when any label is appearing. You are watching for such suggestions: KEEP AWAY FROM CHILDREN, NEVER OPEN BEFORE AN OPEN FIRE.

In the old days we are tossing away the liquid and reserving the cork for a bouquet garni in the beef stew.

saint all rolled into one. Listeners sat spellbound when he spoke, and savored his style of speech with good nature. His lingo was engaging. He never said, "Yesterday I went downtown"; it was always, "Yesterday I am going downtown."

This intriguing talk, a cut above Brooklynese, was labeled (or mislabeled) "historical-present." The delivery fascinated Charlie who thought it was pure entertainment which presented an image as well as any descriptive rhetoric in the English language.

Damon Runyon became the celebrated author-humorist of the '30's, and garnered much of the material for *Guys and Dolls* and *A Slight Case of Murder* at old Lindy's on Broadway (he called it **Mindy's** in his pieces). The 11:30 gathering of characters having morning coffee sprayed cataracts of information that kept everyone in attendance fully abreast of current events: "Harry the Horse," "Nicely-Nicely Johnson," or "Nathan Detroit" dropped juicy items — the latest police bust, the winner of the big pot in the floating crap game, and some matters told only in whisper and nod. Runyon never missed an item.

The topics which generally followed the morning news varied all over the lot. A professor of Botany from CCNY, who was fond of mint, came in to try Lindy's Wednesday luncheon special, Leg o' Lamb with Mint Gravy. He thought the aromatic herb was the perfect complement for lamb, and he was in the throes of extolling the importance of spearmint and peppermint in building the classic Mint Julep when he spied Lindy's pet cat, Mozart. The sight of the beautiful Persian over in her corner, completely relaxed, guided his discourse to yet another member of the mint family "nepeta cataria," - catnip. Runyon was all ears.

The story Runyon published in *Colliers* a couple of issues later was a good piece — a yarn about Big Joe, a country cook in an out-of-the-way tavern who had been surprised with a notification that a very important party would be having dinner that evening. The courier went all out to explain that the guest was as important in this territory as Al Capone was in Chi. Besides, he was somewhat of a gourmet. What to feed the guy? Big Joe had such a thin larder — no sweetbreads, no filet mignons — What about short ribs? Luckily the meal went well. The rolls were warm, the ribs nice and fat and the gravy was plentiful, its aroma alerting all taste buds. The guest made a well in his mound of mashed potatoes, filling it near overflowing, hoping rivulets of gravy wouldn't cascade onto his lap. He was all talk and huzzas about the gravy. The spice wasn't basil, rosemary — he'd never tasted anything so subtle: what was it? Big Joe grinned his widest but never told him it was nepeta cataria.

Song pluggers buzzed around the theatre like locusts. Lads from Remick's, Irving Berlin's, and Shapiro-Bernstein's were out of bed and ready for action, each with a new song or two. Their pitch was short and sweet; it had to be; the two o'clock shows were up and coming. A free dinner, a quart of Gordon's, or a few bucks for a special arrangement — all hard to refuse — were constantly dangled before performers stick-and-carrot fashion. Benefits, going away parties, thank you parties, and party-parties hoped Charlie would attend. And it had to be Charlie, no stand-ins would do. Bob Weitman, Paramount's manager, thought Charlie should go to as many as possible. "Builds your following, good for business." Charlie agreed somewhat but thought in silence that it's those things you do that you don't have to do that kill you. "Not so back in Indianapolis," he said, "we had some time to ourselves."

But the parties **were** really something, and one in particular topped them all. The gal that gave it was a good dame with no stuck-up ideas about how wonderful she was. The boop-poop-a-doop girl who broke the house record at the Indiana sent an invitation to her "Good-Boy" Good-Bye party. Her apartment, somewhere on 66th Street, was comfortable and tastefully furnished, not overcooked as one might have suspected. What a spread: four meats; three fish specialties; six different cheeses including Stilton, Danish Blue, and Roquefort; Italian, rye, limpa and sourdough breads with sweet butter; relishes all over the place, and sweets — count 'em. Charlie wouldn't, he was closing in on 187. Everybody was there discussing the latest flop — not the successes, just the flops. Helen was the perfect hostess; nobody felt lost or out of place or unwelcome. The social arbiters could take lessons from Miss Boop-a-doop. It was a treat to see her bouncing around making sure all stems were filled with bubbly and the trenchermen were brimmed with the heavy stuff.

Charlie had a rehearsal next morning early and cooled it. Anyway, he was engaged in deep conversation with Ed Sullivan whose Sylvia was busily putting on some weight. Ed, a master trencherman and a venerable freeloader, was deep in the Kentucky sour mash, somewhat concerned about tomorrow's column, when some guy broke in, thinking the two of 'em might be prospects for some special value stocks and bonds. Said he'd sold some to the Boop-poop-a-doop girl. He was lying like a trooper; Helen Kane wouldn't buy anything but Liberty Bonds. She had closets full of 'em.

Ed continued to worry about his column. With every worry he had one more drink. With every drink he had one more worry. Finally he took Charlie's arm and whispered that he'd appreciate some help. The next day the following was found in the news room editorial pile, or was it the waste basket?

> Brighton Beach opened yesterday with warm water, warm sun, and bathing-suits so warm that some of the lovelies enjoyed their topless swim. The gendarmes took a dim view after taking a full view... Helen, Boop-poop-a-doop Kane held a shindig for the cast of her show *Good-boy* which closed Saturday. It was a goodie. Her table was a picture. Soft green cloth with blue dishes. A coming combination—blue with green? God thinks so...First time ceviche: raw fish marinated in lime juice, onion, olive oil and dillweed...Wanted to meet Jerry Kern who wrote Goodboy's music but he didn't show...Hoped Charlie Butterworth could've come; was making a movie... hadn't seen Charlie since N.D. days when we roomed together in old Corby...Damon Runyon dropped in for a moment; had to rush to make a deadline for Collier's...Gay Orlova, the Earl Carrol Vanities beauty will marry Lucky Luciano and be deported to Italy along with him. We played her at the Indiana...Hannah Williams of the Williams Sisters act now playing the Paramount is thinking seriously about Jack Dempsy who is ga-ga about her. She'd be #3...Eve Sully of Block & Sully explained why they walked off the bill in Chi. They wouldn't let 'em bill Frank Fay over them, and anyway they wouldn't go on second. They play the Paramount next week...Sylvia Sullivan remarked how long Ed was "paying his dues" before he became a syndicated columnist. It seemed like forever, so Sylvia says...Lou Calabrese will shorten his name to Lou Breese. This fellow is going places, watch him... Lindy's announced a new mustard that goes well on corn-beef between their special rye. I tried it—it's good especially with 3.2% beer now legal.
>
> *By Charlie Davis,*
> *Guest writer*

Parties and still more parties to come — great food, great friends. Sometime or other Charlie's Gang had work to do — work that separates the men from the boys. The New York Paramount would pass the final judgement. "Have you got it, or have you?"

The audience was different. The first three or four rows of kids who came early and stayed late were not there. They were making friends with Russ Columbo, who followed the Gang in Brooklyn, and the down front seats were filled with a sprinkling of nondescripts who came in to enjoy the airconditioning. Most of them didn't know the show was on.

No audience ever got the best of the "Bo" as he was known to his close friends. He wouldn't let 'em. If they didn't like one tap, he gave 'em another, and another. He finally got 'em whooping and hollerin'.

Bill "Bojangles" Robinson finally got to them, but he did an awful lot of plain and fancy dancing to break the ice. A tough audience. Robinson gave the band a chance to accompany the entire gamut of his stock in trade. Ralph Lillard never had such varied demands made upon his drumming. The lads were reminded of the dialogue between the coloratura and the flute. Robinson would tap a series; Ralph's snare would echo. It was fun. The folks couldn't get enough of it, and the rest of the show sold like hotcakes.

NEW YORK BROOKLYN Paramount

New York's Greatest Stage Shows

NEW YORK

Everybody's Joy Friend!
CHARLIE DAVIS
and his sensatole orgorn
in Carnival of youth

EASTER OVERTURE
featuring the Paramount Orchestra

JESSE CRAWFORD
at the Giant organ!

BROOKLYN

Welcome Rudy!
Returning to Br'cairn
A New Rudy New
Songs - New stunts.
RUDY VALLEE
IN PERSON
with His Original Connecticut Yankees!

Featuring
HORTENSE RAGLAND
Personality Girl

IRVIN TALBOT
and Brooklyn Paramount Orchestra

The advertisements never ran out of superlatives.

Kenny Knott and "Coofy" Morrison, in heated argument with the great dancer over the merits and deficiencies of the just announced mid-year models, was a treat rarely experienced. It was the exhaust this; the motor that; the rack and pinion steering raised voices to the highest level since New Year's Eve. Studebaker had come out with a 6 cylinder Roadster, fully equipped, for $895; Nash was about the same, while Chevy had a full page in the New York Times gloryifying its new Roadster at $475. Bo couldn't resist it, "That's a lot of car for the money; I think I'll go for one of 'em." "Coofy", aside to Kenny, "He don't know his ass from his elbow about motors, but he can sure dance."

Why the Swedish Ambassador elected to come during the Saturday rehearsal and stop proceedings on dead center to make a pitch for help in his country's effort to remain neutral in the mini-hassle between Finland and Russia, was a complete mystery to the Davis bandsmen. They didn't even know there was a hassle, or even a back-fence dispute, between two housewives. It became worrisome. Nobody around the theatre had any desire to become embroiled in an incident local, state-wide, nor, for sure, international. But the Ambassador was urgent if not desperate. His plea was fervent and direct. The fellow seemed to get madder and madder at our nation's neglect of the situation, and Charlie thought he was apoplectic, almost foaming at the mouth. The bottom dropped out when manager Bob Weitman introduced the Swede as George Givot, the featured act in the coming week's presentation. For Charlie's special benefit he did his clever Knute Rockne bit. Everyone listened as the great coach, at his after-dinner-speaking-best, told tongue-in-cheek stories and short football quips he used on players: how he was saving one fellow for the Junior Prom, and how his sophomore 140 pounder, Charlie Davis, made a sensational eighty-yard run with the water bucket.

George Givot had 'em in stitches every time he went on. Jokes and gestures, quips and one-liners, with a crazy finishing recitation. The show was a good one; well balanced with Block & Sully, a great team of headliners from the old vaudeville days, and a solid band specialty with Frankie Parrish's "Without A Song" and Harry doing "Minnie the Moocher." Bob Weitman was all smiles.

The cast of *Girl Crazy* had a little party backstage at the Alvin to commemorate the 200th performance of the show. Charlie and Mir Davis had become fond of Ginger Rogers from her appearances at the Indiana and adored the way she sang "Those Songs of Love Are Not For Me," always a favorite Gershwin tune. Ginger wanted to sing it especially for the Davises, but Miriam was back in Indianapolis tending to some family matters: it was her third child and Ginger wished her luck, health, and maybe, for a chaser, a boy.

....

When the news got spread around that Charlie and his Joy Gang were soon leaving Brooklyn, the song pluggers Addie Britt, George Marlow and Benny Bloom set a date for a small informal party they wanted to give the boys for giving them so much play on their stuff. Earle Moss thanked them saying, "We'd have played them anyway...they were good tunes." Nevertheless, they gave quite a shindig at Manny Wolf's. Good food, plenty of schnapps which Manny topped off with Creme d'Cacao and hard-to-get heavy cream.

There was no question, the fellows in the music publishing business were sorry to lose such an easy plug. Charlie had always given them a fair shake, playing no favorites and making sure everyone got the same treatment. George Marlow made the presentation speech as the group gave Charlie a set of diamond studs and cuff links.

"It will be a long time before we meet another bunch of fellows like the Charlie Davis Joy Gang. Far and beyond thanking them for their kindness to us, we thank them for understanding the other fellow's problems. They leave a lot of good friends who will always remember them."

It was a nice talk, and the boys thanked everybody concerned. Just as the group was leaving, Elliot Shapiro called to say that "The Old Spinning Wheel" was an assured hit. "Orders are coming in from all over," he said. He gave Charlie and his bunch the entire credit for "making" the tune.

The next Unit that came in featured Clayton, Jackson, and Durante. Clayton and Jackson were nice guys, and no one would ever throw rocks at them, but they seemed a little like excess baggage. The folks wanted more and more of Jimmy Durante. "The Schnoz" had 'em in the aisles most of the performance. This guy got laughs just by walking. He was funny just putting on his hat. When he played the piano he got laughs, and when he turned that husky voice loose, it was a panic. His famous gesture — looking up into the spotlight, shaking his head, calling attention to the not to be missed schnozzola, his mouth open as if saying "ah" always brought the house down.

Ethel Merman, now being called "The Merm," was happy to meet Charlie again. She spoke of the nice week at Brooklyn where she blasted her way through five shows a day to accommodate the full houses at the Paramount. Her accompanist, Johnny Green, was a friend of Frank Parrish whom he had known for some time. The two of them had an ongoing feud over Johnny's song "Body and Soul." Frankie refused to sing it; said the lyrics were too feminine and should only be sung by a dame. Johnny finally persuaded him to sing the Spanish version. There was some question about Frankie's pronunciation, but nobody blasted him from the Spanish section.

Frankie was in excellent voice. He had set up a program of daily vocalizing, as prescribed by his coach, and noted a decided maturity in his vocal timbre that would qualify him for lead parts in the big shows. It was a great feeling, but other feelings weren't so great. That hydra-headed monster of loneliness continually made its presence known. Frankie joined with the others in wondering what kind of shape the Speedway Golf Course was in. Who would win the coming 500?

The wives would not admit it, but they had like thoughts, paying little or no attention to new cars, baseball games, Brooklyn or the big city, they were secretly anxious only to get back to God's country. They did, however, enjoy the new shows and movies before they hit the hinterlands, and they couldn't decide between Barbara Stanwyck in *'Ten Cents a Dance,* Marlene Dietrich in *Dishonored,* or Ruth Chatterton in *Unfaithful.* It was a problem for them, and the boys were sick about that.

Peg Morris uncovered a *Times* ad which promised a trip around the whole world on the American Dollar Lines; it cost a mere $1250.00 with all expenses paid. She also came up with an offer of eight days in Bermuda for $99.00. Peg said she wasn't suggesting anything...just making mental notes. But mental notes have a way of developing into suggestions, discussions of the relative merits of the French, the Italian, and the North German Lines. The reputations of the *Europa* and the *Bremen* were well known. The food and service rated tens. Mir Davis sent for brochures.

Before any long range plans were allowed to form, however, Charlie checked on things in Indiana. Mom and Pop Davis had kindly offered their help in looking after the Davis kids while the stint in Brooklyn was winding up. He wondered how they were managing. Everyone clustered around the telephone while Mir put through a call. The news was good — all's well, both of them great, and little Jane and Charlene doing fine and missing no one. Mom asked to talk to Fritz about a matter they had been discussing earlier, so he had a chance to tell her how well the Band was doing in Brooklyn and on Broadway, and how Warner Brothers had contracted Charlie to make some shorts.

"Shorts?" Mom Davis questioned, "I didn't know he could sew."

Camera (let it grind)...CUT!

She was a great mom. A little hard on the youngster as she made him practice that horrid hour on the piano while hearing the kids in the commons across the road playing football. But how she could cook! Her cream gravy hand in hand with fried chicken was a classic, and her pumpkin pie could do anything but play the violin. Too bad she never got the hang of doing chili.

Charlie was a fancier of Mexican chili from way back, and he was one of the first regular customers of the Blacker establishment next door to the Ohio Theatre. Wherever he went he spent here and there a wakeful hour seeking out a parlor that would meet his benchmark of high quality. He carefully canvassed the Village, down around Mott Street, a section where Italian specialties were featured; he scoured Broadway thoroughly from Fifth Avenue over to the River but to no avail, and then — right under his nose, a short walk up from the Paramount to 48th and 7th Avenue, he found a little hole in the wall, a chili parlor to top all chili parlors, maybe not in decor, and certainly not in ambience, but it delivered a'table, or rather a'counter with stools, that most satisfying Mexican specialty ever devised, to be cherished by generations of those who love the heavenly pepper.

The El Rancho, if not owned, was operated by a Mr. Strohm, fondly known as Pop. If you happened to arrive at the spot early, a treat was in store. Pop Strohm's entrance was something to applaud, with Inverness cape, lemon-colored gloves, gold-headed walking stick and spats, he would flare into the room prepared to recite any portion of Shakespeare including *Titus Andronicus.* He'd then quick-change to a white uniform complete with freshly laundered apron, asking if you would care for a little more chili to even out the beans and spaghetti in your bowl. Of course, you were having "Chili Three Ways" well-doused with old-fashioned pepper sauce, with here and there an oyster cracker and a well-iced coke.

Charlie enjoyed his bowl of chili most on nights when he was lucky enough to plop down on the stool next to Will Rogers, without question the most notable of the chili fanciers. The fellow took great delight in praising, night after night, the flavor of the dish. "Just the right amount of chili pepper, spices and onion, and the balance of beef, beef heart, and sugar — just right."

Nobody ever challenged his analysis, but then nobody lived as close to San Antonio as Will Rogers did, and that's where the chili came from. It was a treat to hear the legendary philosopher expound. One could hear a pin drop; he held an audience, big or small, like no one else, but seldom sought the spotlight when in conversation with friends. Many were surprised at the dearth of publicity attending his latest venture. Will had just finished a three week tour of the country for the American Red Cross (at his own expense) with his generous effort netting the agency over $9,000 a night. The State of Texas alone swelled the total take by $50,000. The folks urged him to tell something of the tour, but Frank Hawks, the flier who was his partner in these travels, cut him short, mentioning an appointment with Mr. Ziegfeld. Nobody ever kept Mr. Ziegfeld waiting, but Pop Strohm's Chili was something Will couldn't resist. "Pop, I think I'll have another bowl."

....

While the lads in the Davis Band did not actually suffer pains of deprivation as they sweat out Mr. Volstead's mistake, they resented the halter which restricted the satisfaction of their simple tastes. Their attitude, "No goddam bureaucrat is gonna tell me what's good for me and what ain't," led to their seeking out potions of satisfaction — adequate substitutions for the bottled in bond.

The discovery of Tarboro Peach and Jasper Corn caused a polarization in the Band; about fifty-fifty, with a few fellows lacking knowledge of either and unwilling to join in the rhetorical shuttlecock. One fellow, however, took time to make a study of the Tarboro creation — get its history, its formula et al. Coofy Morrison happened to be in the Carolinas calling on relatives, and stopped off in Tarboro asking one of the townsmen, "Where can I buy a bottle of Tarboro Peach?"

The gentleman was friendly enough; "Get yoreself a pitcher or pail," came the recommendation as the fellow warmed considerably, "Mister, you jest walk up thet road over yonder, turn left about ten paces and climb up th' hill; follow yore nose 'bout half a country mile, and when yuh come to a clump of trees you'll see a bright yellow house **with black shutters.**

Thet's the only place around here where you *can't* buy it."

11
encore after encore

It was good news that their favorite funny fellow, Professor Lamberti, would be appearing soon with his xylophone and his ribtickling antics. The Davis boys never forgot his week at the Brooklyn a while back. He tied 'em in knots or murdered 'em, take your pick—and all on account of a simple concoction he'd framed up around the old favorite, "Listen to the Mockingbird." Without a doubt it was a classic. It was a study in byplay between himself and the band's drummer, Ralph Lillard. The Prof would start the chorus:

"Listen to the mockingbird" at which point Ralph's whistle would answer "Tweet....tweet."

And again,

"Listen to the mockingbird." and Ralph again: "Tweet...tweet."

And the finish,

"And the mockingbird is singing"...but no Ralph—he'd missed his cue!

Then, excitedly, the Professor —

"Gimme the bird...gimme the bird!"

Out in the audience somebody actually gave him the bird, a bird so distinct it almost splattered.

The audience wanted encore after encore!

    The boys could hardly wait to see what he'd conjured up this time around. He would present an entirely new act, with a gifted strip-tease artist, who not only had the body, but also the "do you like what you see" look in her eyes. She had elevated the mere removal of an item of little consequence to an art form, and when she knuckled down to the nitty-gritty one could hear the cries of "More! More!" even if they were only telepathic. Professor Lamberti played his xylophone during the entire act, oblivious of her presence.

The audience was completely captivated by the Professor whaling away with his hammers, alternating between difficult arpeggios and beautifully phrased melodies, as Miss Lovely was innocently removing her items of raiment while the gentlemen out front studiously counted her blessings. His grandiose musical climaxes would go completely unnoticed while some of his ordinary fiddling would rate spontaneous applause, especially when the lovely Miss was getting closer to bare facts. The Professor acknowledged gracefully with a smile and a nod. With each cheer he would bow a bit deeper. He took bow after bow, and then more bows. The excitement was building and the applause seemed to dissolve into a groundswell of more...more...more, urgent, demanding. Miss Lovely was willing, but law is law.

The Professor's curtain speech was a gracious thank you with a remark, "You know, in Milwaukee, I did 27 encores."

The Joy Gang hated to admit it, but they were finding new, knockout band specialties harder to come by. Phil Davis wondered if a spinoff of the Bottle Band would be a possibility. After some discussion one of the boys came up with the idea of using a one-note typewriter instead of a bottle. Each lad would ding a note when his turn came, just like he tooted his bottle. The Royal Typewriter Company graciously offered to modify sixteen of their portables to specifications, each to have a differently pitched bell. The theatre agreed to give them a good plug from the stage, and the idea went into rehearsal.

Earle made a beautiful arrangement of "How Deep Is The Ocean," featuring the brass quintet, Frankie sang a chorus with trio background, and the boys down front with typewriters on their knees dinged out the final chorus. The affair laid an ostrich egg. The gang was disappointed. They had a meeting.

The stage electrician came up with an idea. He rigged individual spots to light up each fellow as he dinged his note by punching the key with a short stick which was radium painted. Lighted with ultraviolet spot, the effect was unusual if a little ghastly, but it saved the number from being an out-and-out disaster. However, the Band resolved never to try it again.

The "Pipe Organ bit" went well. The Gang decided to try a different twist on the ultraviolet light stunt (hoping not to go to the well too often). Each lad got himself a pair of white furnace gloves on which he painted piano keys in radium. They formed a circle, their hands sticking out like dog paws, the ultra-violet light hitting them from the booth and voila! there was a pipeorgan manual. Charlie proceeded to play like he was Jesse Crawford. Under his touch, the lads let out oohs like a diapason without tremolo, nasal squeaks like a kinor and muffled eees like the English post horn. The effect was engaging as the simulated pipeorgan performed "Three Little Words" with the melody in diapason, interrupted by embellishments in kinor as Charlie reached for the high notes. The bit, done downstage, looked good, sounded pretty good, and got generous applause from the audience.

Just when the lads were sure they'd never get over the typewriter floppola, something caused a quick turnaround. It had been a well-whispered rumor: Warner's had rented, borrowed or bought the main stage setting of *The Front Page* and were hipped on the idea of a journalistic band specialty. After one of their directors caught the Joy Gang doing the typewriter bit, he started making plans. "Fits like a glove," he decided, and sent the Joy Gang a contract for the guts of the affair. Over in Astoria the whole team thought Charlie and his bunch would be great. Boros Morros fell in love with the idea. Vince Minelli said Warners had a choc'late drop and hoped they'd give up on the idea so Paramount could grab it. But the dates were set, and the dough was on the line.

The boys were disappointed because the producer hadn't let them use Ruby Wright as the girl singer. Ruby could sing rings around the girl they hired, but strange things happen in show biz. Friends have friends and friends of friends have friends and on and on.

Everyone in the band surprised himself and all concerned with his presence on camera. As a group, they reminded one of a dressed-up, grown-up gang of dead-end kids. Karl Vande Walle wasn't too bad doing a Chevalier imitation—chin and all. Phil and Harry had a couple of very funny bits. Coof surprised the director by doing a difficult piece of business with his cornet, causing the guy to remark, "You fellows are pretty good actors—you musta worked Medicine Shows all your lives."

Earle never needed a rehearsal

When do we eat?

Earle Moss was at his composing best when he did the scoring. His arrangements were the source of much comment from the pros around Warner's. "Where'd this guy come from?" Even in the incidental interludes Earle showed his stuff, flashing one back to the days when symphony orchestras cued the silent pictures. Earle's simple but effective theory of scoring made the chore of recording and dubbing a breeze.

To spread the credit for a job well done, the Davis Joy Gang complimented the resourcefulness of the guys at Warners. Anytime the dish started to go a little flat, they were there to spice it up with a shot here and there from their extensive library of pertinent film clips. Their director was patient, not caring how many times a number required rehearsing and shooting. The girl singer wasn't so bad as the guys had thought. Everybody was happy; the film in the can, and the band guys left smiling with pockets full of money.

It was too bad the lads didn't take the work more seriously, a cardinal flaw in group thinking. No matter what facet of the music business they tried, if it wasn't on the stage, it wasn't worthwhile. Charlie remarked time and time again how he felt like a goddam fool standing up in front of the Band with nothing but a grin and a stick. He thought the leader of a band who did nothing but direct was strictly fifth wheel. Take away the job of Master of Ceremonies, playing straight man, and selling the show in general automatically reduced Charlie Davis' value to absolute zero. And that was alright with him. He could quit tomorrow and never walk out on that stage again, and that would be O.K. too.

Fritz Morris could see himself filling molars and extracting wisdoms any time now.

The new Unit, called *Rooftop Review*, had a score with some delightful work for the Band. The Rasch Ballet was one of Madam Albertina's best efforts. Although everybody thought a rooftop should have had dames in shorts instead of tutus. But toe dance they did, and beautifully. Even without lots of skin showing they were the hit of the show.

Morton Downey's personal appearance headlined the Presentation. The poor fellow had a bad cold and could hardly sing because of it, but trooper that he was, nobody knew the difference. He sang his closing number "When Irish Eyes Are Smiling," taking the high C with some effort, but the note came out clear as a bell. Did Morton sound like Kate Smith or did Kate sound like Morton Downey? Put them behind a curtain and let them sing "When the Moon Comes Over the Mountain" and Mister Silverman would put six to five on the morning line from Indianapolis that no one would be able to tell one from the other.

Things were moving right along in the world of 1931: Babe Ruth was hitting at a .387 clip with 127 hits for 328 times at bat. Pretty good for the Bambino. Lefty O'Doul went 1 for 4 over at Ebbett's. President Hoover suggested that Germany buy our wheat and cotton on liberal credit terms. Paris and New York planned $250 millions in credit to Britain..."Where the heck are we getting all this money?" A young fellow named Clark Gable was America's new favorite — he was playing with Norma Shearer in "A Free Soul." Wonder how Hunk Anderson is going to do out at North Dakota since they made him head coach? The alumni fellows didn't think he'd done too badly as interim coach at Notre Dame. Might not be too easy to get a top flight coach to take over. Very likely nobody in the high brackets wants the job...too tough to follow the Rock. Mir and some of the wives caught Georgie Jessel, James Norton, and Fannie Brice in *Sweet and Low.* It was a great show, and they loved Fannie. Good news! The band moves back to Brooklyn week after next.

It was rehearsal morning. Everybody — bandsmen, stage hands, electricians, advertising men, and the projectionists were waiting. The headline attraction, Buddy Rodgers, would be late. He had missed his connection, his plane would be in about noon or shortly thereafter and there would be a four hour wait, at least. The boys sent out for coffee.

Eight o'clock was much too early for a song plugger, but one showed up. Addie Britt, from Shapiro-Bernstein, was hoping the Band could give him a break on his new tune, "The Old Spinning Wheel" — maybe get it in next week's show. He gave his usual pitch — said it would be terrific for Frankie Parrish, and the fiddles could make like a spinning wheel in the background. Few bands had fiddles, and this band, being so equipped, could introduce a sure-fire hit. Earle Moss was all attention. "Gimme the lead sheet," he said and then he disappeared for a couple of hours.

Addie had brought a friend with him, Rudi something or other who was a free-lance writer doing an in-depth study of jazz music. The fellow was a definite know-it-all, making sure to let everyone concerned know he had a wealth of knowledge on his subject. When questioned about his sources and authorities, he made some statements that seemed pretty far out. His instrumental heroes were mostly from New York and vicinity which caused Fritz Morris to wonder whether he'd ever been west of the Hudson. The guy opined, "The only pure jazz is the primitive music of New Orleans. It is the only jazz that is completely faithful to the original idiom." That did it. Charlie blew his top, immediately launching into his "Essay on Jazz" which he delivered with spirit and eclat. The boys in the band got themselves comfortable, as they knew the harangue would last about ten minutes. Addie's friend wished he'd never opened his mouth.

"These statements you make are opinions, pure and simple. They must depend on an agreed definition of jazz. What jazz? New Orleans jazz? Chicago jazz? Dixieland jazz? Sweet jazz? Dirty jazz?...and on and on until someone cries out for a ruling. Those who consider jazz a *musical genre,* a canopy large enough to shelter the many dialects of infectious rhymic poetry, must disagree with such opinions.

"No question the talented black lads from in and around New Orleans deserve their huzzas for the invention of basic jazz music. Most researchers on the subject are ready and willing to beatify, even canonize them for their original creations. But when someone classifies those historic horn-blowings as the only jazz, the pure jazz, and the only faithful jazz, he's gotta be out of his mind. Personally, I must go along with the Duke who says, 'Jazz ain't a matter of color.' He would have no part of the myth, 'If it ain't black, it ain't jazz.'

"But give the blacks even more credit. Let's say they were present at the inception, or call it the dawn of jazz; aren't their contributions to the idiom parallel to the legacy Chaucer and the many anonymes left the early English language when they sang 'sumer is icumen in'? The language changed as did the music. Their originals were at best stones in the rough, with questionable value. It remained for others to cut and polish, finally transforming them into gems to adorn milady's finger, and still others to squire them into the mainstream of worldwide popularity.

"Without the Dixieland Jazz Band's 'Livery Stable Blues,' Miff Mole's trombone, Benny Goodman's clarinet, Bix's cornet, Red Nichols' records with Joe Rushton, and Coon Sanders' nightly broadcasts, jazz might still be back in New Orleans unknown and unsung." The Joy Gang woke up in time to broadcast "Spinning Wheel" late that night from the St. George over a seventy-six station hookup.

All present were glad to see Joe Penner. He was to be on the bill with Buddy Rogers, and he showed up early to rehearse. It didn't take long. Joe was going to do the same act he'd done a few months back, and the boys knew it by heart. They could play it without music. Charlie always liked to play straight-man to Joe's bits. The folks back at the Indiana liked them...no reason they wouldn't do well at the Paramount.

Buddy's act was strictly instrumental. Of course, he gave a short monologue and stood spotlighted in center stage, letting the little girls see how handsome he was and what a nice guy, etc., and how he got to be a movie star. No question about it, he was a heck of a goodlooking kid, and they loved him. His saxophone playing wasn't as good as his looks; his trumpet playing was strictly—forget it—, but like they say, "When they like you, anything you do is O.K."

Buddy closed his act with a flashy bit of drumming. He was all over the lot with his cymbals and tom-toms, climaxing the showoff with the stick throwing bit. He never missed a catch and kept the rhythm going full blast. The front row kids applauded him heavily, as did the "biddies" who would've like to mother him. The rest of the audience applauded with a reserved courtesy that made one wonder if the folks forgot to remove their gloves. Buddy took two bows. One would have been ample.

Since the movie star went on next to close, Joe Penner was moved up to the number two spot. A few minutes after his "wanna buy a duck" entrance he and Charlie did his original restaurant sketch. The bit was just about the right length; Joe sat a'table looking at the menu. Charlie, as the waiter in white apron with pad and pencil, was ready to make suggestions and take Joe's order. "You'll have some of our beets, sir, won't you?"

"No, I don't like beets."
"But we have the very finest beets."
"I never eat beets. I hate the damn things."
"But our beets, sir?"
And so on for quite a spell, bandying beets back and forth with Joe frowning, building his laughs, shaking his head, more laughs, grunting, becoming irritated, and exasperated and finally shouting in desperation, "Waiter, please bring me some beets."
"Sorry, sir, we're out of beets."
The audience loved it.
Bob Weitman cut it. "For Christ's sake, the thing is too strong. Folks came to see Buddy Rogers, and we're goin' to give 'em Buddy Rogers."

Going back to Brooklyn was good. Nothing had changed. It was the same, or was it? Is anything ever the same? No one was reciting lyric poetry out loud, but the band lads were thinking things like, "The blossom drops from the rose, the blush from the youth." The boys would just as soon pack up and leave at once. The excitement of too many times around continually verified the unshakable law of diminishing returns. The kids in the first three rows were there applauding...maybe not quite as much, but still applauding. Charlie wondered if he could hold out a few more weeks; if he could walk out on that stage even one more time.

Phil Davis put a stop to such nonsense, "Let's act like grownups." It was good to have a guy like Phil loose in New York. He was a born instigator, as well as ferreter-outer. He could smell out the worthwhile spots, the recommended culinary delights, the interesting teams, and the fascinating shows. He knew how to put this and that together and come up with a tasteful restorative that the two-fisted trenchermen would loosely call a cocktail. He had researched the advertised nostrums, and passed judgement on the phonies. Phil thought Charlie ought to know about endocrine tablets which could be taken by those unfortunates who would like to fit into velvet pants. Charlie took about $20 worth on his advice, which guaranteed weight would melt away like the winter snows in April. The result as pictured might well have come to pass had not Phil, in the same breath, touted the glory of a place over on

54th Street: Zum's Brauhaus. He painted Zum's in full color: a place that served the most delicious knockwurst and sauerkraut this side of the Atlantic, with German beer reminiscent of the beloved Budweiser Cafe on South Meridian Street in the ol' home town. When they sat about the red-checked table cloths, the Joy Gang sang lustily, drank beer with dedication, and waited in anticipation for that mellow-mix of the grinder, comfortably nestled in a bed of sauerkraut, nee the lowly cabbage, reborn as a lady of distinction.

"Waiter, please, a little horseradish and some dark mustard...and another stein of beer."

Phil's knack for finding interesting eating spots was only one of his prize talents, for he could also hear a band a mile away and tell you whose troop it was...knew which popular arranger was having writer's block, and what singer was flat. He was quick to find spice in the theatre, and he was a veritable bloodhound at sniffing out genuine talent.

"The first time we ever saw her," Phil commented, "she was cute, or maybe darlin' as mom would say, and she didn't get awkward as most kids do when they're in-betweeners." She stayed darlin'. Sylvia Froos, once billed as "The Little Princess of Song" was twenty when she came to Brooklyn. She could sing a song with the best of 'em. The band fellows had a ball from the first rehearsal. They loved listening to her tell of experiences as a child performer· — of her difficulties with the law in Louisiana and Alabama where a child could sing a song, recite, but not move, dance, or even walk, while in the spotlight. One manager had to pay a $25 fine every show she did because some ladies had complained about the little girl's dancing on stage. At four shows a day she got to be somewhat expensive.

Boros Morros was searching for someone to replace Frances Langford, whose material didn't seem to fit in with the special unit the Astoria lads had in rehearsal. Vince Minelli had designed a beautiful set; Phil Boutelje's arrangements were superb, so the head man wasn't about to spare the horses in getting the right songstress. Sylvia Froos was it. The Davis outfit had an opportunity to show its stuff. Coofy, Frankie, and Phil did their trio arrangement of "Tea For Two" which Sylvia embellished with a lovely obligato she'd dreamed up. It's unusual for an audience to applaud a countermelody, or even to recognize one, but this evidently touched a nerve. "Tea for Two" at last count had been done a jillion times, but not that way, and the audience was appreciative. They sometimes know what they like.

The Band fellows liked Sylvia Froos and Sylvia liked them.

The band specialty had the boys doing the tap-dance routine they'd learned from Jack Broderick a couple of years before. They'd practiced several weeks to freshen it up, so the long layoff hadn't hurt any. The folks out front couldn't believe it. How could a bunch of fiddle sawers and horn tooters suddenly turn into Bo Jangles? Borah Minnovitch closed the show with his Harmonica Kids doing the finale from "Orpheus Overture."

Lester's from Chicago phoned the Publix Office to offer a complete set of minstrel costumes that would fit the Davis Gang with few alterations and to suggest that the group could score a tenstrike with a minstrel show like the oldies. "The time is ripe for it," Joe Lester observed as he gave his selling pitch. The boys in Astoria thought it sounded like a good idea. Ruby Cowan, whom they were now calling "the genius," had a basket full of good ideas. The band's own Earle Moss, a minstrel man from long, long ago, had enough ideas to build several full-length shows with two or three units left over. The upshot was a pretty fair, if not good, Al G. Fields copy of the Original Minstrel Show. Phil Davis and Harry Wiliford quickly learned how to apply the burnt cork and become end men. They had considerable trouble keeping the black stuff out of their mustaches, but practice made perfect. It took some time to find an unabridged copy of Joe Miller's *Joke Book.* A new joke was out of the question — nobody could possible invent one. Joe Miller would have to do.

"Who was that lady I saw you with?"

"That wasn't no lady...that was my wife!"

Somebody in the audience heaved a deep sigh, "Oh, no." And that got a laugh.

Charlie as Mister Interlocutor, all dressed up in white silks, ascot tie, white tophat, and white patent leather shoes, holding on tight to keep from going through the floor, kept smiling and doing straight man. When Harry started some untoward acting-up Charlie scolded, "If you don't stop that, I'll have to chastise you."

"My mother had that done to me when I was a baby," — Harry got entirely too big a laugh for such a minor league joke.

"I said chastise, not baptize," Charlie tried to clean it up.

Again, "Oh, no."

It was great fun, however; people loved corn as much as ever, and probably would always love it.

It was not too bad a Minstrel Show....

The Minstrel Show was musically sound. Earle had made a solid vocal arrangement of two songs from "The Prince." Fortunately, the minstrel costumes did not detract from "The Drinking Song" when the Glee Club belted it out, even without the accompanying refreshments implied in the song, but minstrels were notorious for never having enough spare change to buy a drink, so the void went unnoticed. Frankie Parrish soloed "When Irish Eyes Are Smiling," using some of tne vocal tricks he'd learned from a couple of coaching sessions with Morton Downey. He learned to take his high C, hold it a bit, and then do a dramatic flutter down to his finish note which he held while the band built a four bar Irish Fling (fff) into a final cymbal crash. It murdered 'em.

Even the morning outdoor parade was a knockout. The band, the chorus girls, and the cast paraded from the theatre to the Federal Office Building, and every kid in the whole Ocean Avenue district joined in. Traffic was snarled up for a mile. If there had been a fire, the whole district would have been burned to a crisp. Fortunately, there were no accidents, only a hot time. The Borough President welcomed the Minstrels, treating the immense crowd to pink lemonade in paper cups. He must have gotten himself a hundred tousand votes that morning. That week's gross at the Paramount was the third best of all time.

Block & Sully worked in the minstrel atmosphere very well — it was no problem for dyed-in-the-wool troopers; they had scads of material to fit any requirement. Show after show they rattled off new routines that had both the band and the audience in stitches. Eve Sully remarked she'd like to work with the guys on a permanent basis, and Jesse Block, her husband, suggested, "Let's write a show featuring the Davis outfit, have some fun, and make some money." All talk, but no action!

The Joy Gang would be shedding some tears — maybe not big tears, but at least real ones — as the time approached to say goodbye to Brooklyn. Brooklyn made it a farewell duet, for they were saying goodbye to each other. Charlie had not accepted any future bookings; he turned down several attractive offers. Everyone agreed it was quitting time. Everyone was thankful the breakup was completely without hard feelings, rancor, or any of the petty disagreements that often cause splitups.

Ebbett's Field, Church Street, Manny's, Barney Gallants, and Julius's passed in cavalcade as the clock struck. But even fun places fade. It takes people to keep the review alive — folks enjoying the goings-on, applauding, cheering, stomping like twelve year olds, loving every minute the curtain is up — like that group Herman Lieber spoke of; like the dancers that couldn't wait to get on the dance floor at Manitau; like the bunch of Hoosiers that called the Ohio the "friendly theatre;" like the Brooklyn fans — steady, fiercely loyal, brooking no competition with their favorites; allowing no jousting for supremacy in the back yard of their listening pleasure, no outside influence to upset the cameraderie across the footlights. Whether such fans had chips on their shoulders was an open question when the long awaited week at last arrived. The country's number one crowd pleaser was to be the featured attraction: Cab Calloway and His Orchestra would share billing with the Williams Sisters, Jazz Lips Richardson, and Charlie Davis and his Joy Gang. Hannah Williams was the subject of much scuttlebutt, having been seen in various night spots gazing over her Beaujolais with the eyes of a schoolgirl as the ex-champ, Jack Dempsey, pleaded with her to become number three. She was still married to Roger Wolfe Kahn, the band leader, even though she was fed up with him: "He always ran home to his mother any time we had a disagreement." It didn't take long for big Jack and the beautiful Hannah to adjust matters.

But the big deal of the entire season was the coming of Cab. Probably no bunch of musicians in the entire country held Cab Calloway in higher esteem than did the Joy Gang. They learned his tunes, ears stuck inside phonographs; had his mannerisms down to a T; copied his unusual pronunciations, and stole his arrangements note for note. When the Brooklyn Paramount announced Cab's booking, the Davis lads whooped and hollered.

Cab Calloway had a great band, a nice looking bunch of lads that knew their instruments, could play down to a whisper, and ring down thunder from the sky when the *fff* was called for. The Joy Gang enjoyed tossing the fat around with them, congratulating them on their international reputation, and their breaking house record after house record. However, the boys were a little skittish about mentioning that they'd had considerable success with "Minnie the Moocher" — that Harry Dizzy was murdering 'em with it day after day. Coofy speculated, "I'll bet all the tea in China if Cab does 'minnie' the folks out front'll say the sonnabitch is stealin' Harry's song." No one passed this word along, but what difference, the great one would take 'em by storm.

And so he did. Cab's performance held 'em spellbound. He had the young front-rowers on the edge of their seats. The blood brothers and sisters gave him extra loud amens and go-go-goes. Cab's "Minnie the Moocher" was even better than his "St. James Infirmary," a masterpiece by a great artist. The media critics in the front row were scribbling furiously on their pads. Calloway closed his act with a modest thank you speech; he wished everyone well with "Good Luck and Good Health," and waved "see you later."

The news reel which followed was average — nothing to upset anyone. The Organ solo got everyone singing and the lights dimmed down for the stage show. The Publix Unit was a good one. Jazz-Lips Richardson got it off to a fast start with his unusual dance specialty and his Jazz-Lips exit, before going up to his dressing room to think. Jazz always convulsed the band fellows with his "I shall go now and think," as he dramatically sniffed a smidgin of his miracle powder and retired to the second floor. Hannah and Dorothy Williams sang and danced. These sisters had a solid act that always clicked, especially when Hannah did her "Cheerful Little Earful." The folks could easily wee why the ex-champ was nutty about her.

The Albertine Rasch girls were wonderful as usual, and then came the Charlie Davis Band specialty. The gang dressed as usual in their red sweaters, white pants, white shoes, and lugging their white stools and instruments, sort of materialized out of nowhere. They came up stage-center, settled down, and crashed into a medley of pop tunes. Charlie Fach and Phil Davis did a trombone stunt and outdid each other in slipping in and out of the seventh position while playing a series of hot licks in duet. Frankie Parrish sang some Jerome Kern and did the "Serenade" from *The Student Prince* with glee club backing on the second chorus. Earle Moss had written a finale with a Publix ending that really knocked 'em dead, and the boys took bows. The applause was strong and they bowed again. They were just ready to do their about-face hustle back to the bandstand when some little gal in the front row yelled, "Charlie, how about Minnie?" Charlie paid her no attention and, back turned, was making his move upstage when it came again...only more people and louder: "We want Harry," and

"How about Minnie?" Voices multiplied by two and fours, then fours and eights, and finally a gale was brewing into a hurricane. "We got trouble."

But the band hit Harry's introduction. Harry Dizzy came downstage and did his version of Cab's song, and on each *Ho-di-ho* three thousand voices answered, even the folks in the back row, and right on the button, in perfect unison — unbelieveable. It was as if Babe Ruth had hit two home runs at the same time — the yelling, the stomping, the screaming. One's ears will never be the same. The yells of "More! More! More!" stopped the show cold. Charlie couldn't move it. He could have gone home, had a hamburger with onion, and brewed a cup of coffee, but the folks out front were telling the wide, wide world, "You can't play around our rainbarrel; you can't slide down our cellar door...." The kids made sure everybody knew where their loyalties stood.

The Joy Gang got the message. It was a message they'd never forget.

Cab commented, "I never knew the tune was so good."

Cab — the greatest.

12
mish - mash

What is so stark lonely as a theatre gone dark — the show over, the projectionists gone home, nothing but vacant seats, unlighted lights and the leftover scent of people — a place to sit and think things out, if one could stem the urge to slip into that never-neverland with its flashes of gone-byes. Charlie Davis sat third row center, alone with his reminiscences.

The greatest demonstration of spontaneous applause that ever happened in the Brooklyn Paramount came within a whisker of changing a lot of minds, but nothing changed anything. Their thoughts were far from Ocean Avenue, wondering if the grounds-keepers had fixed that sandtrap around the sixth hole at Speedway, if Cal's hamburgers still tasted good with Sammy's home brew? Wondering who could afford these goodies when those nice, fat paychecks came up missing on Fridays?

To hit a golf ball in duet with the hum of a Miller Motor buzzing at a 200 M.P.H. clip was an experience not to be gained at any other spot of fairway. It made a fellow feel like a special Bobby Jones — happy as a clam to have the opportunity to play golf in yet a different atmosphere.

Phil, Reagan, and Kenny had about decided to try an advertising venture that would utilize their talents in arranging and composition. They figured that radio would be a profitable facet of the advertising field, if they could come up with some saleable ideas. Fritz would naturally take up where he'd left off and reenter Dental School. Ralph Lillard had been approached by the Indianapolis Symphony Orchestra to take over as librarian and percussionist, while Ralph Bonham and Art Berry thought they'd fiddle a while longer, although Art had an idea he'd like to go into the insurance business. Frankie Parrish had several offers to join other bands — Abe Lyman would pay him a lot of money, and Frankie was thinking it over. The other fellows were undecided. They were not in a hurry to make a change in their living habits, and even with the uncertainties that go with jobbing, they thought they could do worse.

Mr. Quimby up at Ft. Wayne wanted Charlie to play a few weeks at the new Emboyd Theatre, doing the stage band stunt with some of the local lads. Seymour Weiss of the Roosevelt offered the Blue Room for a stretch, thinking New Orleans would like Charlie Davis for the Mardigras. The Junior Prom at Baton Rouge wondered what a band would cost for the big Spring Weekend at LSU. Elitch's Gardens in Denver called with an offer of a month, and even the Netherland Plaza, the classy hotel in Cincy, thought a band would be a hit on WLW if Charlie'd come for a spell. Offers were indeed plentiful; the avenues many, but he'd have to see. One thing's for certain: there'd be no sixteen Hoosiers in back of him blowing their hearts out, not would there be a thousand hands applauding out front. It would be a new day with *THAT BAND FROM INDIANA* scattered to the four corners of the country.

Charlie's eyelids grew heavier; he scarcely noticed the watchman punching the time clock at the rear of the theatre. Nobody would starve! He could relax and enjoy his breather, and even take time to consider Pop Davis

"...suggesting and advising those who sought
to make their lives well worth the price of living,
and give the right dimension to their thought.

"Concerning our careers there came a caution:
'Don't ever be another's hired hand;
make sure whatever is, your name is on the door
and you own it, if it's just a peanut stand.'"

Never disregarding Pop's advice, Charlie'd always work for himself, but doing what? He had adequate funds. Probably not as many Liberty Bonds as Helen Kane, but enough of them to see him through any low spots. He thought about his promise — a promise apparently made to meet Miriam Browne's conditions, but in reality a decision based on his deep down feeling that music is a young man's business. Playing for the great majority of dancers had been the chore of young musicians, and Charlie Davis had no desire to grow old trying to get with the new hops and twists invented after "Tiger Rag" had long gone out of style.

The darkened theatre settled around him with whispering rattles and now and then a heaving sigh as if it were turning over in bed. Blurring in kaleidoscope, his thoughts dissolved from one to another with no continuity or coherence.

Charlie customarily announced hunger after the last show, and the night of his opening as guest M.C. at the New York Paramount was no different. Mir suggested they go over to the Roosevelt where she'd heard the food was excellent and Guy Lombardo was opening. The food was good. Charlie had a broiled mushroom on toast, and Mir, who was nutty about oysters, had an oyster cocktail. But something happened — a case of morning sickness in the evening.

It was nice to wish Guy good luck on his opening night. He was going great guns. The dancers were all smiles; they liked what they heard, and Guy no longer worried about leaving Chicago's Chez Paree where he was king of the hill. "Make the change," he reasoned, "you gotta move up regardless of how big you were where you'd been." To him it was New York. It had to be.

Mir loved "the sweetest music this side of heaven" with Carmen's wide vibrato, even though the neighboring musicians looked down their noses, calling the sound too "nanny-goatty." Guy could not have cared less. He was determined to play sweet and nanny seasons on end, knowing it sounded good and sold well over the airwaves. Every band in America envied the colossal grosses piled up in the big dancehalls on Guy's personal appearances.

Too bad the Davis St. George broadcasts didn't cause a stir. The extremely light fan mail told the story; stage band music just wasn't tailored for the airwaves. The smart money kept on telling Charlie's lads to quit worrying about stage excellence and concern themselves with what goes into that microphone — not what the people out front were seeing and applauding; but the lads paid little attention to the advice. They voted to stick with something they could handle; why let go of a sure thing? Remember the story of the little dog that looked into the water and saw a bigger bone? To hell with radio.

Maybe they should have called to mind the little dog story when they left $2,700 a week at the Indiana while guys sold apples in the wake of Black Friday. "Was it a good move?" Charlie Skouras had asked them after a year of success and unrest. Nobody could answer. Nobody knew. When Fritz told him the band was breaking up with no plans for the future, the big boss of the Indiana agreed, after considerable thought, "Much better to do it on purpose — no sense in waiting for hard times. The big band is fast becoming a thing of the past. You'll have plenty of time to think things over. Nobody's going anywhere, anyhow.

Mir and Charlie listened attentively, nodding agreement with an occasional "you're so right" thrown in; but as the gentleman left for more important matters, they filed his comments along with yesterday's crop of scuttlebutt.

Night after night they'd sit in one of the back booths at Lindy's listening to characters describe today's incidents as they became tomorrow's headlines. Many a well-known name was dropped in a quick sketch voice that invariably faded before it developed an extended scene. Whispered stories without punchlines and punchlines without stories....

Mir's corned beef on rye without horseradish and mustard continually amazed Charlie who couldn't understand how anybody could forgo the delightful tournament of tastes to be enjoyed by the judicial addition of these simple condiments.

He didn't order a sandwich; he wanted a bowl of chili-mac at El Rancho, where he hoped to run into Will Rogers after his late performance at the New Amsterdam Roof, Charlie never got over being impressed by Will's ability to "invent 'em on the hoof." Amazing how that man could take a current event — something that happened as recently as this morning, and get such timely subject matter into a performance on the same day. Put together with the accuracy of the draftsman — ready for immediate delivery, with emphasis where it should be — it was a unified study in composing precision. Sounds very simple, doesn't it? But in the glare of the spotlight, what a gift ....

"You got it all wrong," Will Rogers stated, raising his voice. "My friend," he said, "nothing I do is ad-lib. I'll get an idea, write it down; rewrite it, and fiddle with it some more. When it seems funny and I like it well enough to use it, I'll practice it in front of a mirror until it feels natural, and then I'll put it into the act." "Nothing I do," he continued, "is done any other way — I'd be scared to death to ad-lib."

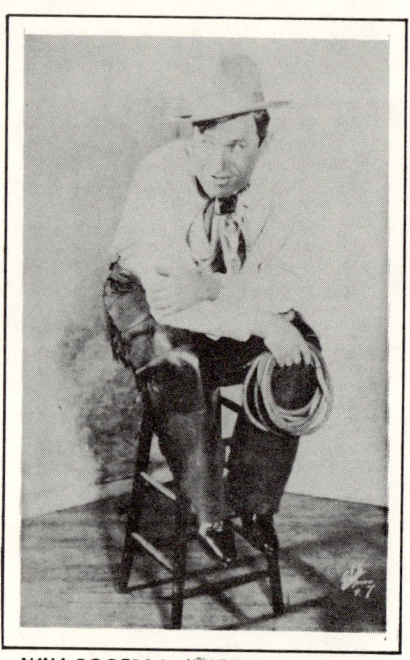

WILL ROGERS in "ZIEGFELD FOLLIES"

It was not strange that the hassle surrounding *impromptu ability* leaked over into the ongoing argument which found bandleaders choosing up sides. Some declared the ad-lib boys — jazz music composed in the playing — did the superior job while others insisted the school of "play 'em like you see 'em" was the only way. The battle had drawn considerable blood, with points made on both sides. Duke Ellington made no bones about insisting the lads in his big band play the notes as scored. He said again and again, "I pay my arranger a lot of bread to make papers sound like something good. I don't want no different ideas gummin' up the tune. If you want to jive," the Duke advised, punching the table with his clenched fist, "get yourself down to Manny's and sit in."

Both Bix and Red thought it best to do a little woodshedding before cutting a record. They had a horror of clinkers — Red Nichols could never suffer the embarrassment of the engineer stopping the recording on account of one of his. Bix subscribed to Samuel Johnson's thoughts on inspirational prayer, and drew a parallel with the jazzmen who prided themselves on their extemporaneous hot choruses:

> "Whatever his intuitive abilities to improvise, he cannot but believe that he himself might compose a better transcription by study and edited ventures that would arise in his mind at sudden call; and if the gift of inspiration be summoned into play, why may he not receive it in private rehearsal as well as in public performance?"

For some time now, Bix had given cause to wonder — a wonder hard to pinpoint, as if the bottom had dropped out of a bucket full of good health, good luck, and good fun. Bix seemed sort of prepossessed, looking out into space and seeing nothing. He coughed more than he should have. He didn't eat like he should have. He drank more hard liquor than he should have. Nothing was the way it should have been. Bix was not the same guy that had murdered 'em with his chorus on "Sweet Sue." The boys in the band had taiked

Bix looked good but wasn't

some of trying to induce Bix to join the Davis group. It was a well-known fact that nobody in this band ever needed AA. Ralph Hayes even offered to try to find another job for himself so that Bix could take over the cornet chair. Charlie rolled it over in his mind for a while, but didn't like the idea of interfering in another fellow's problems.

He wished he had.

- 153 -

The theatre was cool and comfortable, the seats restful, though the red gros point wasn't as soft as velvet, it probably wouldn't wake a fellow up unless he was wearing a bathing suit. But he wasn't, so it didn't.

The old rehearsal room across the alley from the Ohio Theatre was a great place to get away from it all. Mr. Coulter had made the band a present of a beat-up Story & Clark piano, sans ivory, that he said he got for the trucking charges, and warned all concerned not to look a gift horse in the mouth. It did come in handy. Dick Powell learned most of his songs to the accompaniment of the old instrument — after it finally held its tuning. Hoagy made it sound like a million dollars when he played "June Moon" with his right thumb playing the melody and the rest of his fingers doing impossible things that sounded wonderful. He woke up everybody in the adjoining hotel when he lashed into "Junkman Rag" and the guests, instead of giving him hell, yelled "More! More!" The Hoag didn't give 'em more of the same, but rather changed pace, shifting into a lovely melody no one had ever heard. It was a haunting strain written, he said, by Hank Wells, a classmate at I.U. He claimed that Hank gave him a lot of good ideas for melodies and song titles as well as a tremendous lot of inspiration. Hank Wells could inspire anyone. He played a lot of jazz fiddle, could romp all over a piano and write a sensitive lyric along with the best of 'em. He called the song Hoagy was playing "Falling Star." The first line: "Falling star, from afar, you are lonely tonight." A beautiful line, and the star idea was a good one even if it caused the guys down at the University to wonder if the song-poets ever thought of anything other than the stars. Hoagy was fooling around with a ditty he thought of calling "Stardust."

He could play with both hands

Falling Star

[handwritten musical score with lyrics:]

Fall-ing star From a- far You were Lone - ly To-night you were ____ a- lone Just be- fore your flight now when you left the sky did you hear a sigh it was on- ly the an - gels say ing good - bye Falling Star from a- far In my song you will be for your spell as you fell came so sweetly to me now Heaven is smiling they know where you are in my heart to re- main falling Star

    The manuscript of "Falling Star" was found in a box of odds and ends moved from Indianapolis some forty years ago-laid aside and forgotten. Hank Wells, the author, probably scored this lead sheet himself, or if not, dictated it to Peg Morris who jotted it down. Miriam Davis says it is not Peg's handwriting, so it must have been Hank.

    The staff should show one flat as the melody is in the key of F. We, herewith, enter the chord pattern rather than disfigure the manuscript. As we diminish a chord from the bottom the D7dim would be: C, A, F sharp, and D sharp.

F--D7dim--Gmin--C + 5
F--D7dim--Gmin--C7
F--E7dim--C7--C + 5
F--D7--Fmin + 6--C + 5

F--D7dim--Gmin--C + 5
F--D7dim--Gmin--C + 5
F--D7dim--F2/7--D7
Gmin--C7--C + 5--F....

    It was never possible to pin down the actual date "Falling Star" was composed and whether or not it antedated Hoagy's "Stardust" or vice versa but considerable scuttlebut surrounded the **star** theme down at I.U. and many lads wondered who was the inspirer and who the inspiree?

But that was before he latched onto the silver cornet.

He wanted to learn to play the instrument more than anything else in this world. Why the obsession? Nobody knew, but that was Hoagy. Bix told him that people didn't make such sounds in the better drawing rooms, and that he'd never learn to play it the way he was going at it, but the Hoag kept on tooting away with everyone holding his ears, and Bix, for good measure, holding his nose.

He finally got Hoagy to let up on the horn so he could fiddle on the piano. He couldn't concentrate while this outlandish horn tooting was going on, and he was determined to play his new brain child for those who would listen. Having recently become enamoured of augmented fifths parlayed one after the other, Bix elected to cram as many into an eight bar strain a possible even if they made little melodic sense. The "masterpiece" showed definite traces of Debussy, Ravel, and here and there some Cyril Scott. Bix played with considerable grace and finesse, looking up once in a while to see if anyone was smiling a token of esteem. He called his tune "Cloudy." Charlie heard the tune a couple of times and on the third go round put his ear close to the old instrument for one more listen. It wasn't long before he had a lyric:

"Nimbus clowns stroll aimlessly
I see them dim the pale, leftover sun.

Shadows seem to follow me
I wonder why we are worlds apart.

When I ask, 'My Dear, what is our story?'
Shakes her head, 'There is no story.'

It is then
The rain pours into my heart."

Hoagy remarked it wasn't a very good lyric.

"How about the tune?" asked Bix.
"That ain't very good either."

Charlie awakened with a start. The cleaning women had arrived. It was time to go home. Mir would be calling the cops any minute.

Roll Call

Art Berry
Ralph Bonham +
Reagan Carey
Phil Davis
Jack Drummond +
Charlie Fach +
Kenney Knott
Ralph Lillard +
Fritz Morris
Coofy Morrison
Earle Moss
Frankie Parrish +
Karl Vande Walle
Harry Wiliford +
Gene Woods +
Charlie Davis

Karl Vande Walle

Dear Charlie — First please excuse my scribbling — can't see too good (ala Earle Moss — have 2 small cataracts + scar tissue from a detached retina op'n. a few years ago.)

Karl Vande Walle will always be the guy with the baritone saxophone. Even back in the late 20's when the renowned Paul Whiteman did his week at the Indiana Theatre, opening the concert with Charlie Strickfadden's baritone saxophone soloing "Just a Memory", the lads were choosing sides, "Who was the greatest: Strickfadden or Vande Walle?" Karl's haunting tone, however, left a sound-print on one's mind, giving a flavor to the band's timbre that was distinctive.

"And thanks for the quail." Karl's father who could shoot through a needle at a hundred paces, passed a few Seymour, Indiana bobwhite to his close friends each fall. A great gourmet experience for those seeking gourmand status.

The last communique had Karl winning the California Championship as the leading ELECTROLUX salesman. "Come over and do our living room," Mir Davis urged. "Our grandchildren simply rearrange the dust."

REMEMBER WHEN?

1. *You + I went to Louisville's KY. Hotel to hear + hire Dick + we stopped in Seymour + had a real fine chicken dinner by my mother?*

2. *When — Ray Bolger + Phil D. got into a real fight in a school days bit on Ind.*

stage & the audience thought they were just acting.

3. When - I tried to write down all the gags, jokes & poems while we were on stage (behind the scrim?)

4. I always liked this one —
"I wish I was a little egg
Away up in a tree
Away up in my little nest
As bad as I could be.
Then I wish you'd come
& stand beneath the tree
& I would up & burst myself
& splatter thes with me"

5. When - the first couple of weeks in Brooklyn Paramount. You could spot in the audience, people reading the newspaper while we were on — but "Sixty-Nine out of a Hundred wants to be kissed" changed that to instant success. & many benefits.

6. Tillie's Kitchen — coke bottle, a dollar bill & good chicken too.

Charlie any chance of getting out to Calif.? If you can — please give me a ring & will get together & chew the fat about? this & that.
Give my best to Mir. Hope this finds you both well & have a Happy New Year. as ever (but a little older — 79 next 6-3-82 KARL K.

TEL. NO. → (213) 366-5161

Phil Davis

Charlie Davis spent a considerable part of his life viewing the music business as a young man's affair, probably because his father worried through a career of uncertain pay checks. Playing trombone in pit orchestras, his family had steak for dinner, if the theatre had a show. If it was dark: beans, sauerkraut and mashed potato...no meat. Charlie remembered and sought to build on firmer ground.

When THAT BAND FROM INDIANA broke up, however, the lads had no trouble doing well, either in music or out of it. The varied experience proved a worthwhile foundation for any career they chose.

Phil Davis' success in the musical facet of advertising is a case in point. Charlie changed his mind about "music, a young man's business."

EVERY MINUTE OF EVERY DAY*

there is a

PHIL DAVIS MUSICAL COMMERCIAL

on Radio & Television

building sales in every major market for all kinds of products

(*Current Broadcast Schedules average over 22,580 per week)

PHIL DAVIS
MUSICAL ENTERPRISES

MUrray Hill 8-3950
59 East 54 Street   New York 22

Phil Davis musical enterprises, inc.
A CREATIVE MUSICAL SERVICE FOR ADVERTISERS...

RADIO

COMPOSER Phil Davis, in his New York office, at work on the beginnings of the Beneficial musical theme. Here, tune progressed from "one-finger" melody to full piano score.

> *Listen! It's the wonderful sound of money!*
> *Money for the holiday season, Cash for any good reason.*
> *Cash? Just say the word! You're the boss at BENEFICIAL!*
>
> One hot day back in the early summer, a Tin Pan Alley tunesmith got up from his piano with a sheaf of papers in his hand and a lot of music in his head. He had just developed the melody for the "bare" words that would become the Beneficial jingle!
> This man was Phil Davis, songwriter, author of scores of successful pop songs and creator of many outstanding jingles, including Zest Soap's "For the first time in your life, feel really clean;" Schlitz Beer's "Know the real joy of good living... move up to quality, move up to Schlitz;" Carling Ale's "There goes that call again... Hey, Mabel, Black Label."

Art Berry

1932	Joined Waring - Roxy Theater
1934	Indianapolis Symphony
1935	With my own orchestra
1936	Thomas Jefferson Hotel, Birmingham
1937	Claypool Hotel (Atrium Room)
1938-39	Red Gables, Indianapolis
1939	Last six months Washington Hotel (Sapphire Room)
1940-49	Columbia Club - nine years
1950	A few club engagements and I disbanded and quit playing.

I was born in Wabash, Indiana - about 8 miles from LaFountain (Fritz), 20 miles from Marion (Mrs. Davis). Played shows at the Eagles Theatre 1916-18. Came to Indianapolis in 1919. Started to study fiddle in Urbana, Illinois in 1910. During my senior year at Shortridge High, I had my first orchestra in the Bamboo Inn -- after graduation-West Baden and back to the old Crystal Theater on Illinois St. In 1921 Virgi Moore and Emil Seidel asked me to leave my orchestra and join them in the new Apollo Theater. They were such wonderful musicians I left my orchestra and spent a year and a half in that Theater.

Charley Olson told me one day he was giving us competition at the Ohio Theater. A great orchestra - Charley Davis (who?) was going in there. The rest is your history.

In 1936 I started in the insurance business to use up day time. As Red Skelton said "I didn't want to become a Honey-Dew. Honey do this - Honey do that." Had to get the hell out of the house.

Anyway, this is my forty-fifth year in the business, and it has built into something great. I _must_ retire soon.

Thanks for your interest. With best wishes for you and your family.

Sincerely,

Art

ART BERRY INSURANCE

Kenny Knott

After leaving Brooklyn I went to radio station WLW in Cincinnati in February of 1932. I played some piano with other studio musicians for about a year. I also wrote orchestrations for orchestras and vocal accompnaniments for singers. (Doris Day, The Modernaires and others.) I was with WLW until August of 1944 when I left and went to New York. There I wrote orchestrations for radio shows and for records. I left New York in January 1947 and toured the country looking for the place where my wife and I wanted to live. We decided Portland, Oregon was the most beautiful city and Oregon the most beautiful and exciting state. We moved here in 1948. After getting acquainted with musicians and the music situation I had my own band for about 5 years. Tiring of traveling I disbanded the combo and opened a studio where I taught piano for over 20 years. In 1963 I played for a private party given by Conrad Hilton in the new Portland Hilton and then played dinner music with a violinist in the dining room for over 4 years. I continued teaching and playing for parties and banquets. In 1974 Icalled it quits and retired. My wife and I now live in an apartment on a bluff overlooking the Willamette River, downtown Portland and the west side hills and north Portland.

That about covers it, Charlie. I didn't bother to mention playing with various local Orks or that the Indiana Theatre experience allowed me to play for hundreds of floor shows, fairs, rodeos -- you name it -- I was the busiest.

I truly hope that we will be able to see one another again in the not too distant future.

My very best always

Fritz Morris

We came back to Indy in November of 1931, and settled down to what seemed like "country life" after our year in N.Y., and our trip to Europe.

I went back to I.U. Dental school as a Junior, and graduated in June, 1935. I opened my office shortly after, and practiced in the same location forty one happy and productive years.

About the only time I played fiddle for many years, was when Hoagy Carmichael or Hank Wells came to town, or when Charlie came back for a get together with some local musicians.

About ten years ago, I started playing in the Athanaeum orchestra a couple of nights a week, and with a chamber music group once a week.

Our son Tony is a stockbroker with Dean Witter-Reynolds. He has three children — Timothy Toke who is a Junior in Purdue (Engineering), Dania Dawn (stripper name, huh?) who is a music major at Butler (plays piano, flute + piccolo) and Oliver Todd (thirteen years old) who is a professional actor who toured with Tony Randall as "Winthrop" in "Music Man", and with Theodore Bikel in "Sound of Music". He was "Patrick" in "Mame", had the part of "Oliver" in I.R.T. production of "Oliver". He plays piano, trumpet, synthesizer & sings and will continue study in music and theatre.

Our younger son Dave owns his own food brokerage company in Louisville, Ky, and is a gay bachelor ("gay" as in "happy"!)

As of now, I'm recovering from a bout with viral pneumonia, and trying to capitalize on the "gold" in the greatly overrated "Golden Years". The "Silver" years with the Charlie Davis Band were so great, that the "Golden Years" suffer by comparison. However, I'm happy to be here, enjoying retirement and recalling the good years.

Coofy Morrison

Charlie phoned Coof in Florida last year but has since lost track of him. He either owned a Motel or managed one in the sunny state. It's reported he lives with his son somewhere in Indiana.

Coofy, however was the last member of THAT BAND FROM INDIANA to leave Charlie. He did the Hotel New Yorker stint and most of the fill-ins that completed Charlie's ten year pledge to his wife. He cut several records with the band, doing vocals on two that sold well. His "I've Got A Warm Spot In My Heart For You" was especially well received.

Coofy made the western trip with Charlie, doing Elitch's Gardens, the LSU Junior Prom and the hold-over engagement at the Roosevelt Hotel in New Orleans, where he was a great favorite of Senator Hughie Long. The Senator thought he sang "How Deep is the Ocean" just about perfect. Coofy shed real tears when the radio blasted out, "Dr. Carl Weiss shot and killed Hughie Long, Senator."

As a band historian, Coofy Morrison had no equal. He could take one back to the days of Bob and Gail Sherwood at the Alhambra; Virgil Moore and Charlie Lines at the Apollo, and tell how Emil Seidel could play that piano. He could trace growth of supplementary music, when theatres in the ol' town hired lads to play jazz music during the news reels and comedies, and in so doing started something -- something that eventually grew into the style of entertainment this book is all about.

Reagan Carey

I quit playing professionally about 1963 and was appointed Chief Clerk of Marion County. I next served as Chief Bailiff of Marion County Superior Court, Room 1, until 1971. During this period I played 1st. Clarinet in the Murat Shrine band also with the Shrine Dixieland Band. After double eye surgery in 1971 I retired and became assistant to the director of the Audio-Visual Dept. of Indiana-Purdue University at Indianapolis, where I remained part time until 1976. Now, fully retired, I am active in record collecting and have about 1100 original 78 recordings which I make available for Jazz Radio and TV programs, and the Indianapolis Jazz Club. My wife, Lois, being a dedicated jazz buff, assists me in taping numerous Jazz programs and records which we send all over the country. I miss playing a great deal but am having a lot of fun trying to keep the reeds wet.
Kindest regards from us both and love to Mir,

Best wishes for a happy and healthy 1981,

Reagan

Earle Moss

Earle Moss gets extra coverage in this section because he was a lot of people at the same time. He was an instrumentalist: third trumpet and fourth sax when needed, as well as Barnhardt's Gin Mixer. In his ever-so-spare moments he was arranger, composer of incidental music while still overseeing the mix on Barnhardt's Gin. And on top of that his spots of wit and humor qualified him court jester.

Earle was the last member with whom Charlie had musical contact. He accepted the challenge to arrange a score for Charlie's composition written for Oswego's 100th birthday celebration. A Pageant "Let Flow The River" had nine songs and considerable incidental music. Earle wasn't sure he could see well enough to undertake the commission, but he did, with excellent results. The Oswego AFM Band under the baton of a misplaced Hoosier from Greencastle Indiana, the late Weldon (Slim) Grose, played the score; St. Joseph's Choir sang the vocals; the Fort Ontario Guards did their gun routine, and the State University at Oswego's stage-craft students did the lighting.

So "Thanks, Earle."

It can be told now, I guess but down in the Indiana basement before the 2nd newsreel of the afternoon. I often had a visit from Fritz. He would sneak into my arranging cubicle in the manner of a spy in those who-dun-it TV shows and after latching the door, would say in a stage whisper, "Are you holding anything?" I used to keep a gallon jug of gin in my desk drawer and would proffer it to him. He would take a good swig, then would ask, "Do you happen to have any Clorets or Sen-Sen? I don't want Bonham or Berry to smell my breath." I had to add Clorets and Sen-Sen to my office equipment.

When THAT BAND FROM INDIANA disbanded, Earle moved into the top echelon of national arrangers as he joined the Radio City Music Hall team, producing scores that gave the large orchestra a desirable swing-band sound.

Erno Rapee and his successors gave Earle credit for many show-stopping presentations over a period of 19 years. Earle often remarked, "It looked like a steady job."

We reprint a news item from 1932:

Arranging for CBS radio and various recording artists came after the bands. Red Nichols was one of the performers for whom Moss arranged.

Then, in 1932, a man named Erno Rapee contacted Moss about an arranging job. Moss decided to accept Rapee's job offer and asked where the job would be.

"It is going to be at one of the biggest theaters in the world," Rapee said, "and it will be called 'The Radio City Music Hall.'"

Moss started working before the theater opened. He had never arranged for an orchestra as large as the one at the Music Hall was to be. The orchestra was a symphony-type orchestra which was scheduled to play popular music, something completely new.

"I couldn't help but wonder to myself, if I would be able to make pop orchestrations for that big band," Moss said.

Make them he did, however to the satisfaction of Rapee and also to the satisfaction of the great George Gershwin whose "Second Prelude" he converted into a blues number for the Music Hall's prima ballerina, Nina Whitney.

The ballet pianist took Moss' arrangement to Gershwin who looked it over thoroughly. The pianist asked Gershwin if he had any suggestions or changes to make, and the great American jazz musician said,

"Don't change a note; it's fine."

"For the rest of the day, after I heard his comment, I felt as good as if I had just gotten a raise in pay," Moss said.

Going hand in hand with the great melodies of the tune-filled twenties were the equally great lyrics of the era. Masters of the rhyme and metaphor queued after Oscar Hammerstein, Irving Berlin, Larry Hart, and Gus Kahn to fashion outstanding marriages of melody and message.

- Big Ed East sang about Elephants
- Lou Blank Solid Drummer good baritone
- Loren Griffith anchor man of the Glee Club
- Ralph Dumke sang Capt. Andy in "Show Boat"
- Coofy Morrison Senator Huey Long's favorite singer.
- Ruby Wright one of the first girl singers
- Cy Milders killed 'em at the OHIO
- Louie Lowe discovered the "Vagabond Lover"
- Mel Snyder good banjo "I never Realized"
- Frankie Parrish a sensation over W.L.W.
- Dick Powell graduated into Stardom

That Band from Indiana sensed the importance of the lyric from its beginning in the field of dance music, and was markedly successful in engaging fellows who could deliver lyrics as well as sing melodies. Above are those outstanding entertainers who did yeoman's service in the ten years covered in this book.

CLOUDY

by Bix Beiderbecke
as remembered by Charlie Davis

Nim--bus clowns stroll aim-less-ly I see them blot the pale left O--ver sun
Soon the clear-ing skies will fol-low as the rain clouds fade and dis ap--pear

Shad--ows seem to fol-low me I won why are we worlds a----part
Could be we should try to get to--gether One more time one more start

When I ask My Dear "what is our sto--ry and she says to me, "There is no sto--ry
When I ask My Dear, "is there a mo--ment and she says to me, "This is our mo--ment

It is then the rain pours in-to my HEART................
It is then a song pours in-to my HEART................

This page is included as an afterthought. Since the ambitious documentary "BIX" filmed by the C.B.C's producer, Brigette Berman, has been shown around and about, Bix's tune "CLOUDY" has stirred up considerable interest, with numerous requests for the score and lyrics. Played as a piano solo by this writer in the documentary, the melody is found only in the haze of his total recall and inclusion in "THAT BAND FROM INDIANA" seems the best way to rescue it from the unknown.